D1246217

ONE GOOD TURN

SARAH M. SCHLEIMER

FELDHEIM PUBLISHERS
Jerusalem ✡ New York

First published 1990

**Library of Congress
Cataloging-in-Publication Data**

Schleimer, Sarah.
    One good turn / Sarah Schleimer.
    144 p. 21.5 cm.
    Summary: On their way to Israel, a Russian-
    Jewish family spends some time in England
    where teenage Nadja blossoms into
    maturity as she lives a free Jewish life and
    makes rewarding new friendships.
    ISBN 0-87306-527-1.
    ISBN 0-87306-528-X (pbk.)
PZ7.S346940n   1990
[Fic]—dc20   89-71536
                             CIP
                              AC

Feldheim Publishers Ltd.
POB 6525 / Jerusalem, Israel

Philipp Feldheim Inc.
200 Airport Executive Park
Spring Valley, NY 10977

Typeset at Astronel, Jerusalem

Printed in Israel

This book is dedicated
to our People throughout the world
who are not yet free.

1

THE MONDAY MORNING that Nadja Letchkov first walked through the gates of Batsheva High School for Girls was a warm and bright one in mid-April. From the tops of trees bursting with fragrant blossoms, birds sang their sweet melodies, heralding the arrival of spring and a new beginning. Girls seemed to swarm from all directions, walking together in groups as they laughed and talked excitedly about events that had taken place over the Pesach holidays. But Nadja walked alone for she knew no one there.

It was just over two weeks now since she had arrived in England from the Soviet Union with her parents, two brothers and little sister. After eight years of waiting, they were finally permitted to leave and were given their exit visas. Their original intention had been to go and live in Israel immediately. However, the post that had been offered to Nadja's father, a top medical consultant, was not yet available; the doctor who still held the position had not yet retired, although he was due to do so shortly. For this reason, Dr. Letchkov had decided to accept a temporary post in England until the one in Israel became available. In the meantime he would learn to speak *Ivrit* fluently, so that when they eventually arrived in Israel he would be able to practice medicine immediately.

For Nadja, just the freedom of being able to do as she pleased, when she pleased, was a gift in itself. And being able to go to a Jewish school — this was like a dream come true. In Russia, up until only recently, she remembered, if Jews wanted to have a *Seder*, it usually had to be done secretly lest the authorities discover them and arrest them for sedition. Obtaining kosher *matzos* had been virtually impossible.

This Pesach, her first spent in the West, had held great meaning for her. As the *Haggadah* related the ancient story of the Jews' liberation from bondage, Nadja had felt that her own personal story was being recounted. She thanked *Hashem* with all her heart for allowing her and her family to be free, and for being able to celebrate Pesach properly.

At first, life in England had seemed strange to her: it was totally different from what she was used to. The language barrier was also a great problem: she understood and read English, but spoke a "broken" version, very slowly, which embarrassed her and made her reluctant to speak. Her father assured her, though, that she would soon master it. Another problem was that because she had never attended a Jewish school, she was not as advanced in Hebrew and Jewish studies as the other girls of her age would be.

These worries filled Nadja's thoughts as she walked through the gates and down the narrow path leading to the school building, and she suddenly felt extremely nervous and shy. She did not know any of the girls, and could not talk easily to anyone. Nevertheless, Nadja was a fighter; she vowed to study as hard as she could until her English was up to a good standard, and she was determined to somehow make new friends. Nadja knew that she had been given a wonderful opportunity and she intended to use it to the best of her ability.

2

NADJA TOOK a deep breath and walked through the main entrance into the school. Girls of all sizes seemed to be running everywhere. Nadja had been told that the school was quite small, but it was far larger than she had expected it to be, and she could feel what little confidence she had slowly vanishing. However, it was still not as large as her old school in the Soviet Union had been. She thought of that tall and imposing coeducational State school with its small concrete playground, so unlike Batsheva High with its attractive, two-story building surrounded by a large courtyard and playing fields.

Nadja looked around. Ahead of her rose a large, wide staircase, and, to her left and right, corridors. She wondered which way she was supposed to go. Her father had said something about seeing the headmistress, but Nadja had no idea where she could be found.

After wandering about for a while, she found she was not getting anywhere and would have to do what she so dreaded — ask someone to help her. Nadja approached a tall girl with long, light brown hair tied back in a high ponytail, and a mass of freckles covering her small nose. She was engrossed in reading the notice-board. Nadja cleared her throat, and was about to speak when she realized that she hadn't the faintest idea what she was going to say. As she collected her thoughts she hovered anxiously around the girl, trying to work out how she was going to catch her attention, when suddenly the girl turned around and asked, "Is something wrong?"

"Please…where is…headmistress office?"

"Turn left and walk straight until you reach the end of the corridor, then turn right and it's the second door on your right," she replied, smiling brightly.

"So," Nadja began, trying to repeat the rapid instructions, "I go left…and it is second door."

"Well, not quite." The girl checked her watch and then told Nadja, "You know what, I'll take you there myself."

On the way to the office, they struck up a conversation. "Are you new?"

"Yes, I am…new," Nadja replied.

"What is your name?"

"My name in Russian is Nadja, but I…want more to be called Nava."

"In Russian? Do you come from the Soviet Union?"

"Yes."

"Really? Well, *Shalom aleichem*, Nava! It's lovely to meet you. I hope you'll enjoy it here in school and if you want someone to take you around, I'll be happy to do it.

By the way, my name is Rachel Nachshon. Do you know what class you're going to be in?"

"No...but I am...thirteen."

"Then you'll probably be in Form Three, the same as I. Here we are already. This is the office."

"Thank you, Rachel, very much...for help."

Nadja paused before knocking on the dark wooden door. While talking to Rachel she had stopped feeling nervous, but the prospect of talking to the headmistress — whom she had only met once before — caused the uneasiness to return. She gave a hesitant, light tap.

"Enter!" came the reply.

Nadja turned to Rachel with a perplexed look on her face. "She means 'come in,'" Rachel explained.

Nadja slowly opened the door and haltingly walked in.

"Hello, Nadja. *Shalom aleichem*, and welcome to Batsheva High School," said Mrs. Gera, looking up from the papers that were scattered across her desk. The warm blue eyes which shone from her kindly, middle-aged face sparkled with pleasure. She was so different from Nadja's old headmistress back in the Soviet Union — a short, stocky woman who was extremely strict and always seemed to be in a foul mood. "How are you and your family settling down in England?"

"We are...fine."

"I'm happy to hear it, but if you do run into difficulties or have any problems, please don't hesitate to come to me. I will be more than happy to help you."

"Thank you for this...kindness, Madame."

"I hope you will enjoy yourself here, Nadja."

"I am…certain of this, but please to call me by the Hebrew name, *Nava*."

Mrs. Gera smiled. "With pleasure. Now then, Nava, you had better run along to class. The bell will ring in a few minutes and after registration there is assembly. I'm sure you will find the girls very helpful and friendly, but I will try to come in anyway, at some point during the day, just to see how you are getting on."

"Uh…Mrs. Gera?"

"Yes, Nava?"

"Mrs. Gera…what class I am in please?"

Mrs. Gera tapped her head and gave a sigh. "Nava, I'm terribly sorry — I completely forgot to tell you. You are in Form Three. Do you know where to find it?"

"No, but is girl outside…Rachel…she knows."

"That's fine then. Remember, Nava, I am always here if you need me."

Nava nodded and left the office, to find that Rachel was still waiting for her. "You have…got now a…new class member," she told her, smiling shyly.

Rachel took her to their classroom. "Would you like to sit next to me?" she asked.

"Yes…very much," Nava replied. She was pleased that she at least had someone to sit next to and would not have to sit on her own. Nava put her bag down on the floor beside her and sat on the edge of her seat, watching all the other girls milling around. Would the rest be as kind as Rachel? she wondered. Are they friendly? Will they accept me? Will they like me? She wondered whether she was, after all, the fighter she had originally thought.

That morning, before she had come to school, she had visualized how she would walk into class and start talking to everyone immediately, without having any problems about what to say. In reality, though, she was not terribly good at making friends or talking to people she didn't know, and all she could do was sit there feeling alone.

While she was feeling sorry for herself, one of her new classmates walked past, her nose buried in a book so that only her copper hair was visible over the top of it. Somehow managing to notice Nava, she shut her book and said, "Hello! Are you going to be in our class?"

"Yes," Nava replied.

"How nice to meet you. My name is Chaya Touren."

"Mine is Nava Letchkov."

"Where are you…?"

"Hi! *Shalom aleichem.* I'm Sharon Metzer," burst in a vivacious girl with blonde hair and almond-shaped green eyes.

"I am very pleased to…meet you."

While Nava was getting acquainted with Chaya and Sharon, another girl came over to her, but Nava could not quite catch her name. Shortly afterwards a fourth girl came to join them, and then a fifth, and soon the whole class had come to welcome her — all twenty-five of them. Nava was left with a blur of names and faces, and the feeling that they were a very friendly bunch.

For Nava, assembly was amazing: the first thing they did was *daven*. Back in the Soviet Union, assembly would have begun with the singing of national songs. Now the most important part of assembly was expressing daily gratitude to Hashem. After the prayers, Mrs. Gera formally welcomed her to the school. Although it was a very thoughtful gesture, it embarrassed Nava so much that she felt herself blushing.

While filing out of assembly, Nava studied her timetable. There were four different lessons listed for first period and she could not figure out which one she was to attend, and where it was to be held. Nava did not relish the thought of walking into her very first lesson late; it would not be an appropriate way of starting her new school.

"Having any trouble?" Rachel asked her.

"I do not understand…timetable. What lesson I must go to now?"

"It depends on what you put down on your choices."

"Choices?"

"We made choices at the end of last year about what subjects we wanted to take this year, but I suppose you haven't been given them yet."

"So what to do?"

"I suppose you should go to the lesson in whatever subject you wish to take."

"But I wish to take two."

"Then you can take one in another pool."

"A pool?"

"For our choices we were given four pools, with four subjects in each pool. We had to choose one subject from each pool."

"Four pools in subject? I do not understand."

"I'll tell you what — come with me for this lesson and we'll go to Mrs. Gera afterwards. She'll help you sort out your choices." Since Nava had no idea what to do, she went along with Rachel, hoping that she was not expected somewhere else.

After consultation with Mrs. Gera, the rest of the day passed smoothly. Now that Nava had her choices worked out, all she had to concentrate on were the lessons themselves. Her new friends helped her as much as possible and Nava soon discovered that, aside from problems in understanding some of the English, she did not find the lessons themselves too difficult.

That night, while packing her school bag in preparation for the next day, Nava realized that for the first time in her life she had enjoyed school. She did not have to worry about being bullied or teased there, just because she was Jewish. There was no need to wonder how she was going to ward off the gangs on her way to and from school. That night, crazy as it seemed to her, she was actually looking forward to school the next day.

3

IT WAS ALREADY FRIDAY! Nava could hardly believe it. The week had flown by and she had thoroughly enjoyed it — even all the homework. She was adjusting extremely well to her new "free" life, and both her English and Hebrew were improving steadily.

The bell rang: it was lunchtime. Nava grabbed her packed lunch and went to join the other girls sitting outside in the playground.

"Hey, Nava, we're over here!" someone called. Nava could just make out Chaya's profile in the bright sunshine. She was sitting on the grass with Rachel and Sharon. Nava joined them and settled down to enjoy her salad.

"Would you like to come with us to group tomorrow?" Rachel asked.

Nava gave her a puzzled look and did not know what to answer. She did not even know what "group" was, but could she tell them that? Would it make her look like a fool? They seemed to assume that she knew what it meant, she reasoned, and so it must be something that everyone knew about. Nava could just manage an "Uh, well..."

"Don't you think you'll be able to come?" Sharon asked.

Nava felt a little uneasy; her three friends were looking at her, waiting for an answer. Nava thought that perhaps she should simply say "Yes," but on second thought, what was the use of saying "Yes" if she did not even know what she was agreeing to?

She took a deep breath. "Please do not think me...foolish," she said, "but...I do not know what...is 'group.'"

"Oh! I'm really sorry," Rachel replied. "I should have explained. Group is what we go to on Shabbos afternoon. We all go either to the group's own meeting house or to a person's house who belongs to the group. We have a group leader, a *madrichah*, who organizes all sorts of activities for us. We have discussions and sometimes we sing songs. Do you think that you'll be able to come?"

"It sounds very nice. I will ask my mother tonight."

That night, Nava's face shone as she told her mother all about group. Mrs. Letchkov, who had been worried about her daughter's adjustment to life in England, was as delighted as Nava and told her that of course she could go, "with pleasure."

On Shabbos afternoon Nava waited impatiently for her friends to arrive. That morning when she had seen Chaya in *shul* and told her that she would be able to come to group, Chaya was very happy and Nava even more so. It felt good to be accepted so warmly and so soon.

There was a knock at the door: there stood Rachel, Sharon and Chaya. After bidding a hasty "Good Shabbos" to her mother, Nava headed off to group with them.

On arriving, she saw many of her new friends from school, and also a few other girls whom she did not know. She assumed they went to other schools. Sharon introduced Nava to the *madrichah*, whose name was Naomi. Naomi was a pretty and very friendly girl whom Nava estimated to be about eighteen. She was rather petite and her long blond hair was held back in an intricately designed hair clip. Her yellow dress, Nava thought, matched her hair almost perfectly in color. She reminded Nava very much of someone she had known, her best friend back in Moscow, Olga.

After some time for socializing, they all sat down to hear what Naomi had in store for them that afternoon.

"Good Shabbos to you all," she began, smiling at all the seated girls. "I think we will start off with a discussion. Why do you think that it is important to keep all the *mitzvos* in the Torah? Isn't it enough to merely acknowledge the fact that we are Jewish and to be proud of our heritage? Rachel, perhaps you would like to start. What do you think?"

"Well," Rachel said with conviction, "besides the fact that we are commanded to keep all the *mitzvos* and therefore do not really have a choice in the matter, I think that the Torah is our special heritage, and if we don't keep it, then we are not much different from the other nations of the world."

"And if we don't keep the Torah," Chaya interjected, "we become lost to Judaism and are sooner or later part of the other nations of the world."

"But there are plenty of Jewish people in the world who are not practicing Jews, yet they remain Jewish and are recognized as Jews," Sharon argued.

"True, but sometimes they marry out and become lost to Judaism," Rachel replied.

"Why do you think that Jewish people sometimes abandon the Torah?" Naomi asked.

"Oh, for lots of different reasons," Rachel began. "During the war, for example, children were left with non-Jewish families and forgot about being Jewish because they had been away from a Jewish environment for so long. And then hardship and poverty are other reasons: they can make people feel that the only way to scrape together a living is to work seven days a week, and gradually more and more things get forgotten. And then sometimes parents work so hard and spend so little time at home that they don't see how their children are turning out."

"Yes, these are some of the reasons," Naomi agreed. "Nava, what do you think?"

Nava looked around at all the faces waiting to hear what she had to say, and she was suddenly overcome by self-consciousness about her Russian accent and broken English. But she *did* have something to say. She took a shaky breath. "Well...I come from Soviet Union as most of you know. There are many Jewish people who hardly know...what means Jewish, but still there are some who are coming back to…Judaism. I think when people are…free, do not so much think about who they are. They see what other people are doing and think, this is better life, so…they do what other people are doing and try to become…like them. I think there is word in English for this, no?"

"Assimilation?" Naomi suggested.

"Yes, yes, that is it. In Soviet Union, people are not free, so they…stay together and not give up what is theirs, because it is only thing they have. You have here freedom that people in Soviet Union have never seen, only dream of. Until month ago I too…dreamt…of …freedom." Her large brown eyes brimmed with tears and her words began to falter.

"You don't have to continue if you don't want to," Naomi said softly.

"No, no. I want to. I must. I want you to know what is life there…really. Until only…short time ago, our life was so very hard. Since new government is now, there is…better feeling, and more freedom for Jewish people, but is very…slow and will be many years before we are…accepted and allowed to…live religion properly.

"In Moscow we live in horrible gray…apartment like thousands of others. There are no houses there. The whole city is gray. Everyone…looks the same, wearing same dull colors. Only now does this begin to change. Young people do not…be foolish in the street, and laugh. I mean, this is not forbidden, but the whole …feeling is…tense and you cannot.

"Sometimes was not enough food and we waited in long line for it. But we always tried to keep happy.

Sometimes, was hard to do…so hard, but always we tried to live in hope. When we wanted to make…a *Seder*, was in secret. It was not allowed to have Jewish books, but one day a man from England came, and…was bringing some Jewish books for us. The day we got all the books, how I remember…we all were crying. He also gave me…picture of *Yerushalayim*, which was my dearest…treasure.

"Eight years ago my father…applied to authorities to leave Soviet Union. He is very special doctor…very clever…but after this, he lost his job. He had no work. The only work he could find was street cleaner. But this is not only problem. Often my father was followed by K.G.B. — secret police. At school…they made joke of me because I am Jewish. Of course I was proud to be Jewish…but sometimes, it was so…difficult. Sometimes I was feeling I had no longer hope, but I knew this cannot be because without hope, one cannot live.

"One afternoon my family and I went for a walk. We come back and saw our apartment is upside down and all our Jewish books were gone — it was K.G.B. They call our books Zionist propoganda! And what books? *Siddur, Chumash*, and book of pictures of Israel.

"But we are lucky! Some of our friends were arrested and put in jail, and some were sent to…Siberia. Some of them sit in jail for ten years. Such a difficult-…struggle is this for us. At last…a month ago, we got permission to leave. And, it is strange…I was happy, yet sad. So many people…left…my friends…and my…grand…" She could go on no longer and broke down in uncontrollable sobs.

"It's all right, we understand," Naomi said, rushing to her and putting a comforting arm around her shoulders.

"So many people...are left," Nava wept.

"We know, we know."

That night Rachel thought about what Nava had told them all. She found it almost impossible to imagine the Letchkovs' suffering. Here was a real family, with a girl her own age, who had gone through so much in pursuit of their dream to live full Jewish lives in *Eretz Yisrael*. It was one thing to talk about Soviet Jewry in class, or to go to a rally and wave a few banners round. But to hear firsthand what a girl like herself went through...

Sometimes I don't realize how lucky I am, she thought. I have such freedom, and most of the time I simply take it for granted. Nava has led such a difficult life. She has suffered so much in such a short time, but today I have learned a valuable lesson: Never take anything for granted. Everything is precious — everything is a wonderful gift from Hashem.

4

IT WAS MONDAY AGAIN — a lovely weekend had ended, and another week of school was beginning for Nava. The sun shone brightly, but looks could be deceiving. It was actually quite chilly and Nava was glad she had taken her sweater. While walking down Orange Drive, she admired the beautiful white houses with their lush, green, well-tended gardens. She glanced at the driveways with at least one gleaming car parked in them. Her house was nothing like the ones on this road, but she did not mind at all. It was warm, comfortable and just roomy enough for six people. With a little bit of work, it would soon look very presentable. They had been in their house in Blossom Grove, Greenhill, for scarcely a month and already her father had painted the whole exterior, and was now working on the dining room as well.

Nava entered her classroom only to find that pandemonium had broken out. The girls were all jumping up and down, shouting happily, waving pieces of paper and every so often crying out the name, "Tree-Glade."

While Nava stood watching this bewildering scene, Rachel rushed up to her, breathless with excitement. "It's so fantastic!" she exclaimed. "We're going to Tree-Glade for *Lag Ba-Omer* again!"

"What is that?" Nava asked.

"*Lag Ba-Omer* is the time when the students of Rabbi Akiva…"

"No, I do not mean, what is *Lag Ba-Omer*. This, I know. I mean, what is…Tree-Glade?'

"Oh, Tree-Glade! Tree-Glade is a really big forest out in the country, a few miles away from Greenhill. We went there last year. First we had a long hike, only stopping for lunch, and then — as the sun was setting — we lit a huge bonfire and sang and danced around it. Oh, it was wonderful! I'm sure we'll do the same this year."

"This sounds very pleasant."

"It is. One of the girls just brought in the information sheets about it. I took one for you too."

"Thank you very much."

"Two weeks and one day to go!" Rachel called, and then bounded off to tell Chaya, who had also just walked in.

Nava rushed through the last part of her homework and finally slammed her books shut. Now she could set about compiling a list of all the items she would need for the *Lag Ba-Omer* outing. As this was her first one ever, she wanted it to be absolutely perfect. When she had completed her list, she found that she was able to come up with everything except a camera. That very afternoon she had passed the local camera shop, and had seen the perfect answer. There was only one problem: it cost twenty pounds. Nava counted up all her savings but all she could muster was fifteen pounds. How could she possibly make up the rest in just two short weeks? She contemplated asking her mother for the money, and knew that she would agree, but Nava just couldn't bring herself to do that. They were having enough financial difficulties as it was, and Nava had no idea when she would be able to pay her mother back.

"Nava, are you ready to go yet?" her mother called from downstairs.

"Go where?" Nava asked, jolted out of her reverie.

"Don't tell me you have forgotten. This morning you told Mrs. Ravman that you would look after her children for a little while this evening."

Nava had forgotten. After quickly pulling a brush through her long ponytail and straightening her ribbon, she raced downstairs. "I am going right now."

"Thank you so much for coming at such short notice," Mrs. Ravman said. "I should have called you earlier, but I was so busy with the plans for Uri's birthday party that I only remembered this morning that I still had to buy him his present. I hope I didn't make you late for school when I called."

"No, not at all," Nava assured her.

"Good, I'm glad." Mrs. Ravman straightened out her blue headscarf, which had begun to slide down her smooth forehead. "Now, the children are all asleep, even Uri, though he was so excited about his birthday that I had a hard time getting him to bed. There is food and drink for you in the kitchen; just make yourself at home. I'll be gone for about two hours. I decided that I might as well do the weekly shopping at the same time. It saves me carting the children to the supermarket tomorrow, and I can take them to the park instead. I'll see you later."

" 'Bye."

Nava sat herself down on a chair in the living room and leafed through one of the magazines that were neatly stacked in the rack beside her. All the while she pondered the question of how she was going to find those five pounds for the camera.

The two hours seemed to race by, and it was not long before she heard the front door open.

"Hi! I'm home," Mrs. Ravman called. "How were the children?"

"Just fine."

"No one woke up?"

"No."

"Good! That means that they'll wake up nice and early tomorrow. And now that I've done all the shopping we can have a great day out. I might even take them to the zoo if it's good weather. I'll just stack everything into the kitchen cupboard and then see you to your gate. I know you only live four doors away, but it is quite late."

When Nava had finished collecting her belongings, Mrs. Ravman reappeared from the immaculate kitchen. In her hand she held a crisp five-pound note.

"Here," she said to Nava. "Thanks so much for your help."

Nava stared at the five-pound note, unsure of whether to accept it or not. It looked so tempting; and it would enable her to buy the camera. Here was the solution to her problem, but would it be right to take it? What had she done to deserve it? All she had done was sit and leaf through magazines for a couple of hours. However, she felt just as shy about refusing the offer as accepting it. She stood there awkwardly for a moment, before finally deciding that she should graciously decline it. "No, really," she began. "It is not necessary."

"It certainly is," Mrs. Ravman replied. "You did something for me, and I am very grateful. This is my way of saying 'thank you.' I quite often have babysitters, and I always pay them. Why should you be any different, Nava? Here, take the money and buy yourself something nice with it."

Before Nava had time to protest further, Mrs. Ravman thrust the money into her hand and propelled her to the front door.

5

AT NINE-THIRTY on the morning of *Lag Ba-Omer*, twenty-six exuberant Form Three girls boarded the school bus which would take them to Tree-Glade. They were armed for the journey with backpacks containing lunches, canteens, cameras, transistor radios and other "essential" equipment. Everyone was scrambling madly to reach the back of the bus. From what Nava could gather, the back seat was supposed to be the best one and, even though she did not understand why, she joined the race to get there.

Over the din, Nava thought that she heard her name being called. She looked up and saw Sharon signaling her. "Nava!" she called. "I've saved you a seat at the back." Nava continued to make her way to the back; now that she had a seat, there was no need to hurry. She sat down next to Sharon, grateful for her friend's thoughtfulness: not because she had saved her the prized seat, but because she had bothered to think of saving her one at all.

As they left the city, Miss Rimon recited *tefillas ha-derech*, the travelers' prayer: "May it be Your will, Hashem, that You…make us reach our desired destination…may You rescue us from…every foe…and evil animals along the way…" At the conclusion of the prayer, all the girls answered, "Amen," and then settled down for the journey, full of high spirits and song.

After an hour's drive, the bus drew up at Tree-Glade, accompanied by the sound of loud applause and cheering. Then the mad rush began again — this time to get off the bus. The two teachers who were accompanying them, Miss Tovim and Miss Rimon, gathered the class together, first for roll call and then to hear Miss Tovim's annual warning lecture. It was the same on every outing, and a few groans could be heard from the audience as the slight, fair-skinned teacher with short ginger hair began.

"Now remember, girls — we stick together the whole day. The forest is big and not the sort of place you would like to be left alone in. Stay only on the marked paths. No rubbish is to be left lying around in the forest. At lunchtime keep all your rubbish together and when everyone is finished, someone will come around with a bag to collect it. Is everyone ready?"

"Yes," they all said together.

"All right then, let's go."

They all hoisted their backpacks onto their backs and began the hike through Tree-Glade. Nava walked with Rachel, Chaya, Sharon and another classmate whose name was Naama. Naama was a beautiful, dark-skinned Israeli girl with black, curly hair and dark brown eyes. Her father had come to England on business and she was now spending her second and final year there. Nava had recently become very friendly with her, feeling a kinship in the fact that they were both new to the school, that neither of them were native English-speakers, and that they would both be going to Israel: Naama to return home, and Nava to "return home" for the first time.

Somehow they got onto the subject of brothers and sisters, and Naama began to tell them about her brother. "Do you know, my little brother is such a pest," she said. "Do you have any brothers or sisters, Nava?"

"Yes. I have two brothers and one sister."

"So then you know what having a pest for a brother is like?"

"Well, not really. My two brothers...are older than me, so are not really pests, but they do...boss me sometimes...though."

"How old is your sister?"

"She is three years." Nava smiled lovingly as she spoke of her.

"And what is she like?"

"She is very sweet, and mostly is...very good. How old is your brother?"

"Well, the little brat, Shimon, is eight, but I also have three other brothers. One is fifteen and the other two are twins, two years old and adorable."

"Why do you find your brother such a pest?" asked Chaya who, being an only child, could not understand how someone could not get along with her own brother.

"Oh, he's always doing ridiculous things, especially to annoy us," Naama replied. "For instance, he is forever walking backwards like this…" she said, impersonating him. "We always tell him that it is a stupid thing to do and that one day something dangerous might happen to him, but does he listen?"

Suddenly Nava opened her mouth to call out a warning, but Naama was too busy demonstrating her brother's walk to notice. By the time Nava could shout, "Naama!" it had already happened. Naama tripped and fell backwards into a shallow, marshy pool full of thick mud and green slime. For a moment she lay there stunned and caked in mud, her hair plastered to her face and topped with ribbons of green slimy plants. Futhermore, she was soaked to the skin.

Naama looked down at herself and, seeing the unfortunate state she was in, burst out laughing. The rest of the group, unable to control themselves any longer, did the same. They were laughing so hard that they failed to notice Miss Tovim, who was now standing right beside them.

"What is going on here? Naama, what on earth are you doing?"

"Well," Naama began, trying to keep a straight face, "I…tripped and…kind of fell into this pool."

"So why are you just sitting there? Get out quickly; otherwise you will catch a terrible chill. It is not summer yet, you know."

Naama attempted to climb out, only to find that her feet were stuck fast to the muddy bottom of the pool. "I guess this is my punishment for speaking *lashon hara* about my brother," she said. "Could someone help me out please?" Sharon took her hand and gave a pull, but still she did not budge. Rachel grabbed her other arm and with one mighty heave, they yanked her out. Once on dry land, Naama suddenly realized that one of her running shoes was missing. Nava stuck her hand into the pool and fished around for it. After a few moments she exclaimed, "I've found something!" Everyone waited in anticipation as she struggled to pull out her discovery. However, it was not Naama's sneaker at all, but an old rubber boot.

Once again, everyone had a bout of hysterics, and even Miss Tovim saw the funny side of it. After groping around in the mud again, Nava managed to retrieve the sneaker, but it was not really in a fit state to be worn.

"What am I going to do now?" Naama moaned.

"Well, for one thing, you can borrow my sweater," Chaya suggested. "I've got a long-sleeved blouse on and I'm warm."

Naama gratefully accepted Chaya's sweater; nevertheless, it did not solve the problem of her skirt or sneakers.

"We're stopping for lunch in a little while," Miss Tovim said. "Then we can all figure out what to do about your clothes."

"But how can I continue? I can't walk in these muddy sneakers."

"Then you'll just have to walk in your socks."

It was only a ten-minute walk to the lunch stop. Once there, Naama was able to clean out her sneakers and wring out her skirt — and her hair. Although she had to sit in her wet skirt all through lunch, it dried within an hour or so.

Once everyone had eaten and *bentched*, they were off again for the second part of the hike.

27

6

"W E'LL MAKE THE CAMPFIRE HERE," Miss Rimon announced. They had only just arrived at the clearing in the woods, and had barely had time to put their backpacks down — much less sit and rest for a while — before the teachers were giving orders again.

"Now, will you fifteen please go and collect twigs and branches to make the fire, and the rest of you stay here, look for stones to put around the spot where the fire is to be, and then arrange them." Nava and Chaya were among the girls chosen by Miss Rimon to collect the wood.

The sun was slowly beginning to dip behind the trees as the fifteen of them went back into the dense forest together to gather some timber. The birds sang their cheerful song in perfect harmony and the trees swayed in the gentle late afternoon breeze.

The girls worked efficiently, and half an hour later they had a large, roaring fire going. "Come, let's dance," Miss Tovim said. Nava sat down on the grass a short distance away and watched as her friends formed a large ring and danced around the fire, singing Hebrew songs. She felt tears of happiness begin to well up in her eyes as she looked at her classmates twirling and singing; it was a beautiful sight. The golden hue of the sky, together with the flickering glow of the lapping flames, was reflected on the girls' faces, making the scene appear dreamlike and magical.

Chaya broke away from the ring and sat down beside Nava. "Are you enjoying yourself?" she asked.

"Yes, very much. It is so very pretty, I must take photo."

"Good idea! I think I'll take one too." Chaya rummaged through her backpack for her camera, but…"Oh, no!"

"What is wrong?"

"My camera — I can't find it."

"You have searched well?"

"Yes. It must have fallen out earlier while we were collecting the wood. I seem to have a hole at the bottom of my bag — the stitching is ripped. I'll run back quickly to look for it. Be back in a minute."

"Okay. I hope you find it."

"So do I."

Just then, Sharon called, "Nava, come and dance!"

"Oh, I don't think…I'm not very good at this dancing."

"Come on."

"Yes, come on, Nava," Rachel called.

"Well…all right, but please to go slowly." Nava joined the circle between Rachel and Sharon, feeling a little clumsy and self-conscious.

"Do what I do," Rachel instructed her. "Go to the left…now to the right…toward the center."

The more she danced, the easier it became and Nava quickly got the feel of it and began to enjoy herself. She already knew many of the songs from group.

They danced until they were so exhausted they could barely stand. "Let's sit down for a while," Miss Rimon suggested, collapsing onto the ground, "and we can sing around the fire." She was out of breath and her wavy brown hair clung to her damp cheeks. As they began to sing, accompanied by Michal on the guitar, Rachel whispered to Nava, "I don't know how Michal managed to lug that around with her all day."

"You are right," Nava replied. "It was for me enough trouble with my backpack."

The sun was setting and the fire was gradually dying down. "It's getting late," Miss Tovim said. "I think we should start heading back. The bus must be here already."

"Make sure the fire is out, collect your things and we'll go," Miss Rimon said.

A few of the girls sighed; they had had such a wonderful time and it seemed a pity that it all had to end so soon. Once everyone was ready and assembled, they took the path to the right for a ten-minute walk to the edge of the forest where the bus was waiting for them.

Before they boarded the bus, Miss Tovim quickly took the roll call. "I think I had better take it again," she said when it was completed. "Someone appears to be missing. Please answer when I call your name."

"Chaya!" Nava cried. "It's Chaya!"

"What do you mean?" Miss Rimon asked.

"She...she lost camera and went back to search in the place where we collected the...wood for fire. She told me that she will only be a few moments, and I did not think anymore about it. I let her go. Oh, how could I forget?"

"We had better return and look for her. Sharon, tell the bus driver to wait for us."

They trudged back down the path silently. "Now, we are all to stick together," Miss Rimon announced firmly. "I don't want anyone else getting lost."

When they reached the clearing it was almost dark. Gray rain clouds were gathering overhead and a chilly wind had begun to blow.

"Nava, where exactly did you collect the wood for the fire?" Miss Tovim asked.

"We especially stayed near to the clearing so that we will not get lost and also because we knew that we will have to keep coming backwards and forwards. We collect wood there, between those trees," she replied faintly.

"She must be somewhere around here then. Let's comb this site."

They spread out over the area, weaving through tall tress, searching in bushes and thick undergrowth. They called Chaya's name constantly but the only answer they received in return was an echo that ran through the forest.

"Perhaps she was here already, did not find her

camera and then went back to the clearing," Miss Rimon suggested.

"Maybe she is lost," Rachel said, despair creeping into her voice.

"Perhaps she is waiting at the bus for us," Sharon added hopefully.

"What do you think we should do?" Miss Tovim asked, turning to Miss Rimon.

"I suggest that we split into two groups. You take half the class and I'll take the other half. One half can wait at the bus for her, and check the clearing again on the way, while the other can keep searching," Miss Rimon replied.

"Do you want to wait at the bus?"

"All right. And we can scour the area around there as well, while we are waiting."

The class divided up. Nava stayed with Miss Tovim to help with the search. However, this time they did not stray too far from the clearing because it was almost dark. Half an hour's intensive searching passed with no sign of Chaya. Suddenly, lightning tore across the darkened sky and rain began to pour down. It became pitch black and, with no lights to guide them through the forest, they were unable to see a thing. The two groups met up once again.

"It's no use," Miss Tovim told the girls. "We can't find her and we cannot even continue to search for her, much as I know you all want to; it's just too dark. With the rain coming down like this, and no proper protection, it's not safe for us to be out in the forest either. We don't even have a flashlight."

"Are you suggesting that we go back? Without her?"

"I don't think that we have any other alternative. If we stay here, the rest of the girls' parents will become worried. We should get back as quickly as possible to notify the police and leave it in their hands; they will have a much better chance of finding Chaya than we will."

"But we cannot leave her here!" Nava cried.

"I'm sorry Nava," Miss Tovim replied firmly. "But we cannot stay here either. We must go back. Please try not to worry. She must have taken a wrong turn on the path. The police will find her. Come on girls, let's hurry onto the bus."

7

THE ATMOSPHERE ABOARD the bus was one of gloom and despair. The girls huddled together, shivering as much from fear as from the chill of their rain-soaked clothing. Nava stared out of the window and it seemed to her that with every passing minute the rain grew heavier. The storm that was raging showed no signs of abating either. Nava felt so anxious — so guilty and frightened — that she did not know what to do. She felt frightened about what had become of Chaya, and guilty because she believed herself to be the cause of it all. After all, she had been the one to let her go back into the forbidding forest alone, against the rules. And she hadn't even noticed that Chaya didn't return!

Nava imagined that all her friends would blame her for what had happened. "Only just arrived in the country and already causing trouble. We will hold you responsible if anything has happened to her," they would say. And the teachers! Although Miss Tovim and

Miss Rimon had not said anything yet, Nava was certain that they still would. When the headmistress found out, Nava would surely be in serious trouble. And Chaya's parents: What would they say? "What an irresponsible friend! Because of her thoughtlessness our daughter, our only daughter, is missing." And her own parents: How would she face them after this?

Worst of all, what if something dreadful had happened to Chaya, God forbid? What if she was not ever found? What if she was found and was...? Nava could not even bare to think of it. How could she live with herself? All this was too much for her. She broke down, tears streaming down her face. She had never in her life felt so helpless and miserable.

"Nava?" Rachel said softly.

"You...must hate...me," Nava sobbed.

"What are you talking about?"

"All this...it is all my fault...if not for me, Chaya would still be here."

"Don't be silly, Nava! Of course it's not your fault. You musn't blame yourself. Even if she had not told you where she was going, it still would have happened."

"But it is my fault, because I...let her go."

"How were you supposed to know that this would happen? Anyway, how could you have stopped her?"

"I should have gone together with her, or at least to tell her to say to a teacher that she goes."

"No, she herself should have known better than to go off without telling a teacher. And what would have happened if you had gone with her? Both of you would have been lost."

"At least she would not be now alone."

"Perhaps, but it would not have helped her or you very much. Now you can at least help find her."

"We should not have left her now alone in the forest."

"And what could we have done had we stayed there? We couldn't even see to look for her. The teachers were right."

"We could perhaps have tried more."

"We did try, and we had no success. By staying longer we would only have made our parents worry. The quicker we get back, the quicker we can fetch help."

"I suppose you are right."

"You know I am, and *b'ezras Hashem* she will be found safe and well."

The journey took longer than usual in the rainstorm. The roads were treacherous, and street lights were continually going out; it was like a nightmare. When they arrived back at school, all the parents were waiting anxiously for them — including Chaya's.

"Where have you been so long?" one mother exclaimed.

"We have a bit of a problem," Miss Rimon began hesitantly, and then proceeded to tell them what had occurred.

"No, no!" cried Chaya's mother, her usually bright face suddenly pale and distraught. "What are we going to do?"

"The police must be notified immediately," said Mr. Touren, Chaya's father. "I will go and telephone them right now."

"Miss Tovim is on the phone with them in the school office," Miss Rimon said.

Mr. Touren hurried off in the direction of the office and returned a few minutes later with a grave expression on his face.

"Well?" Mrs. Touren asked anxiously. "What happened? What did they say? Will they start searching for Chaya right away? Please tell me."

"Elisheva…"

"Yes?"

"They will not be able to help us tonight."

"What do you mean?" Mrs. Touren's voice was barely a whisper.

"The constable I spoke with said that due to the storm, there had been so many emergencies that the police department could not spare us any men. I explained that she had already been missing for some time and he told me that, according to police procedure, it was too early to send out a search party, that we would have to wait at least twenty-four hours. When I said that it could be dangerous for her to be alone in the forest, especially on a night like this, he just replied that if she went off on her own in the first place, she must have known what she was doing."

"Oh, no, what are we going to do?"

"I don't know, Elisheva," Mr. Touren said with despair. "Without the help of the police what *can* we do?"

"Our daughter, our only daughter," wailed Mrs. Touren, "out all alone in the forest tonight. My poor little Chaya, she must be terrified. We cannot wait until tomorrow; it might be too late then."

Nava walked over to where her parents stood. "Papa," she said urgently in rapid Russian, "we must do something."

"I don't see that there is much we can do. We will just have to wait until tomorrow."

"We can't! Look how worried Chaya's parents are. And Chaya is out there all on her own in that huge forest. I still feel responsible for what has happened."

"But Nava, be reasonable. What do you suggest we do?"

"We must go back immediately and organize our own search party."

"What, tonight?"

"Yes, tonight! You and all the other fathers can go, and I will come as well. We can bring flashlights and waterproof clothing and go looking for her. Papa, she has been such a good friend to me. I cannot allow her to stay there, in this storm, in the dark, all by herself."

Dr. Letchkov regarded his daughter quietly for a moment. Then he spoke.

"You are right, Nava." He turned to the others and told them of Nava's suggestion. "What do the rest of you think?"

The other fathers turned to each other and then nodded their approval. "We'll go."

"But Nava," her father told her, "you must stay here. It could become dangerous and it's going to be a very long night."

"Please, please let me come," she pleaded. "I want to come. I have to come. And besides, I can show you the area where we collected the firewood."

"I don't know. What do you think?" he said to Nava's mother.

"As long as she stays with you, she should be fine. She'll be as safe as any of you," she replied.

"All right, Nava, you can come."

Half an hour later all the girls' fathers and Nava were ready to leave. Equipped now with protective clothing and flashlights, and all praying quietly for Chaya's safety, they began the convoy back to Tree-Glade.

8

CHAYA WAS IN A desperate state. She had left Nava a few hours earlier, thinking that she would simply return to the area where they had collected the wood, find her camera and then rejoin the dancing. However, things did not quite turn out that way, and now, as she fought to control her mounting panic, her mind flew back to the start of it all...

Chaya walked confidently back into the dense forest, the towering trees almost obscuring the setting sun. She wove in and out among the thick trunks, heading deeper and deeper into the forest toward the spot where they had collected the firewood just a short while earlier. After about a quarter of an hour she realized that something must be wrong. Earlier, it had taken only five minutes to discover a suitable spot. Now she had been walking for fifteen minutes and still hadn't found it. The area looked slightly familiar, but then the entire forest did, so she could not be sure. If only they had stayed close to the paths when they had gone in search of wood, everything would be so much simpler now.

Chaya now knew that it would be useless to keep on walking since she was getting nowhere. She decided to retrace her steps back to the clearing, before Nava and all the others started to worry about her. When she got back, she would ask them to come and help her find the camera. She headed back to the clearing through the trees, bushes and thick undergrowth but, try as she might, she could not find her way back. She walked for five minutes, which soon turned into ten minutes, and then fifteen minutes, but it was all to no avail; she merely seemed to be roaming still further into the ominously darkening forest. She continued for another twenty minutes, trying to recall the way by which she had come, but it was hopeless. Chaya began to panic.

"Nava!" she shouted, and heard her voice echo back to her thinly. "Nava!" she repeated, calling with even greater urgency. But no reply came. She continued to trudge through the forest shouting every so often, "Nava!" "Rachel!" "Sharon!" "Naama!" "Can anybody hear me?" "Miss Tovim!" "Miss Rimon!" The frantic pounding of her heart seemed so thunderous to her ears that she almost let herself believe the sound of it alone would somehow lead them to her side. Her knees shook; her stomach felt queasy; and the tips of her toes tingled painfully.

Storm clouds gathered overhead, bringing with them an early darkness. The words of Miss Tovim's lecture that morning came back to her now: *The forest is big... not the sort of place you would like to be left alone in... stay only on the paths... not the sort of place you would like to be left in . . . the forest is big.*" Chaya shivered in her thin blouse. She had not yet reclaimed the sweater she had lent to Naama that morning after her fall into the marshy pool. Remembering that moment, Chaya smiled despite herself.

The storm came without warning. Lightning tore across the sky, illuminating the entire forest. Thunder shook the trees, and the ground trembled beneath Chaya's feet. Rain gushed from the sky in torrents, soaking her completely within moments. It was almost dark now, and the little she could see was obstructed by the heavy rain. "Nava!" she called again, but she knew that it was useless. The class had in all probability given up the search for her by now — if indeed they had tried at all. And even if they were still hunting, her shout sounded more like a whisper amid the tumult of the ferocious storm.

As the lightning struck once again, illuminating the forest in an eerie flash, Chaya could see the trees sway-ing to and fro threateningly. "I will not cry," she told herself. "I will stay calm. Everything will be fine. Soon I'll find the clearing where the class will be waiting for me. In a short while I'll be on the bus on my way home and it will not be long until I am in dry clothes with a nice warm drink." Nonetheless, deep down she knew that all she was doing was trying to give herself false reassurance. "Think realistically. You are alone, in a hopeless and dangerous situation. You should not have gone off on your own without telling a teacher, and now you have no one to blame but yourself."

It was pitch black. Chaya plodded on, the repeated

flashes of lightning giving her some indication as to where she was and what was ahead. Words her mother had once said to her ran through her mind now: "Never go out in an electric storm if you can help it, but if you are ever caught in one, remember: do not take shelter under a tree. It can be very dangerous." She trembled fearfully at the thought — there was no place she could be now *except* under a tree; she was surrounded by a whole forest of them! Somewhere not too far away she heard a tree creak, snap and come crashing down, frightening her more than ever.

She suddenly thought of the words from *Tehillim* that her family sang around the Shabbos table every week at *se'udah shelishis*: *Gam ki elech b'gei tzalmaves* — Even though I walk through the valley of the shadow of death, I will fear no evil: for You are with me.

The words gave Chaya strength, and she struggled to stay upright against the force of the storm. The howling wind made eerie sounds as it blew through the trees. *I will fear no evil: for You are with me.* The rain began to fall with even greater force as the fierce tempest raged on. Chaya's sodden red hair was plastered to her face. The ground had become marshy, and when she was not attempting to pull her feet out of the swampy mud, she was trying to prevent herself from slipping and falling in it.

She suddenly wondered if there were animals in the forest. Wolves or foxes perhaps? *May You rescue us from...evil animals along the way...* These words in *tefillas ha-derech* had always brought a smile to her lips, but now they took on real meaning.

43

She could envisage how the lightning would strike and suddenly illuminate there before her a large wolf, its glittering eyes staring at her threateningly. It would growl and bare its teeth, and then leap toward her, and in the returning darkness Chaya would scream…

"Stop it!" she scolded herself. "Stop thinking such morbid thoughts." Chaya tried to comfort herself by singing, but her voice was barely audible above the storm. "Ohhh!" she screamed suddenly, as her feet gave way and she fell face down in the mud. Slowly she picked herself up, freezing, soaking and completely covered in mud. "I will not cry. I will stay calm," she murmured over and over. She refused to give up, and trudged on.

She tried to think of good things, cheering things: the funny look on Naama's face after she had fallen into the pool. What a sight! But…pools? Rivers? What if there were pools or rivers nearby? If Chaya were to fall into one now, *chas v'shalom*… "Stop it! Stop it!"

Her summer vacation — what a memorable one it had been. Her first time on an airplane, her first time in *Eretz Yisrael*. Golden *Yerushalayim*, the hot summer sun, endless clear blue skies and the sparkling sea.

Lightning struck again. She forced her memories: Tall palm trees, beautiful and strange new views, rocky hillsides…

The thunder roared. Desperately, she brought to mind the faces of her family, her dear parents, so caring and loving, all her close friends…what would Nava, Rachel and Sharon be doing now?

Chaya tripped and fell. A sharp pain stabbed her

ankle and she cried out in agony. A flash of lightning revealed that she had tripped on a sharp boulder that was jutting out of the ground. She tried to stand up but was unable to; the pain in her right leg was so intense that she could hardly move it. She forced herself to crawl along — one arm forward, then the other, one leg forward, then the other. She dragged herself along the spongy ground, leaving one of her sneakers far behind. The pain in her leg was so severe that she winced with every movement. It was all she could do to keep from crying out. The rain and wind slowed her down until she was barely moving at all. Lightning struck a nearby tree, and Chaya watched in horror as it snapped in half like a weak matchstick. The tree began to plummet and Chaya could see that it was heading in her direction. She tried desperately to drag herself away from the danger zone, but it was too late: the tree crashed to the ground on top of her.

Chaya lay there, motionless.

9

THE CONVOY OF CARS drew nearer and nearer to Tree-Glade. Nava sat in the back of her father's car, fidgeting nervously and watching the rainy blur of lights and signposts all along the route. The rhythmic sound of the windshield wipers steadied her troubled thoughts a little. The car halted at some traffic lights and Nava's father turned around to face her.

"Nava," he began, "I don't mean to dash your hopes, but I really don't think we will be able to find her tonight."

"I know, but we have to at least *try*."

"We will, but I just don't want you to be too hopeful." The lights changed and the car drove off into complete darkness. Up ahead, all the street lights had gone out.

With one mile to go, Nava offered up a silent *tefillah* to Hashem. "Please Hashem, let us find Chaya tonight and please let her be safe. She has been such a wonderful friend to me. She made me feel so welcome, and I feel that I have repaid her kindness by letting her become lost in the forest. I know people keep telling me that it was not my fault, but I still feel guilty. Please, Hashem, forgive me and let Chaya forgive me as well."

"Nava?"

"Yes?"

"Nava, we are here."

Nava clambered out of the car to brave the elements. She had the advantage, though, of rubber boots, a raincoat and a flashlight; she shuddered to think of poor Chaya. Within five minutes everyone had arrived. Mr. Touren looked ashen and distraught. He stared up at the tall, swaying trees, and Nava could guess what he was thinking.

Mr. Metzer — Sharon's father — began. "As there are twenty-six of us, plus Nava, I suggest that we divide ourselves up into five groups." He reminded Nava very much of Sharon. Both had the same outgoing personality and the ability to lead others. "We'll all move out in separate directions. That way a larger area will be covered, and we will have more chance of finding Chaya." By now he was almost shouting to make himself heard above the storm.

"How will we let each other know if we find her?" Dr. Letchkov asked.

"Shout, as loudly as you can," Mr. Metzer replied lamely, aware of the fact that they were indeed shouting now in order to make themselves heard.

"We will never be able to hear each other in the forest tonight."

"True, but look, the main thing is that we find her. Once we have accomplished that, we can worry about how to alert everyone else."

"Yes, yes," Mr. Touren murmured. It was the first time he had spoken since their arrival.

Once they assembled into small search parties, Mr. Metzer, who appeared to have taken command, directed everyone. The group to which Nava and her father were assigned was to comb the expanse around the clearing. The other members of their party were Mr. Sherim (Naama's father), Rachel's father and two other men, Mr. Mendle and Mr. Schlumm.

The walk to the clearing only took about half an hour, allowing for hazards along the way. Nava trailed closely behind her father, moving almost as if she were a sleepwalker or a zombie — following, looking staight ahead, silent. Her one and only thought was for Chaya: how she was faring and if indeed they would be able to find her tonight. Their pace was swift even under such severe conditions, and Nava struggled to keep up. Everything became a haze to her: tall swaying treetops, thick dark trunks, rain, lightning and flashlights all merged into one.

"Nava?'"

All this is my fault, she was thinking. If it had not been for me...

"Nava, are you feeling all right?" her father asked.

Nava snapped out of her trance. "Oh...oh, yes, I'm fine," she replied.

"I think we have arrived at the clearing. Is this it?

Do you recognize it?"

The flashlight's beam shone over the area and Nava peered around carefully. A few stray, damp branches lay scattered on the ground where the fire had been. Nava's eyes blurred: The fire glowed, someone strummed away at a guitar, girls were singing together, dancing, laughing...

"Nava, is this the clearing?" her father asked again, jarring her from her reverie.

Nava scrutinized the site yet again. There was no fire, no girls, no music — just a miserable reminder of it all. "Yes," she replied with a sigh, "this is the clearing."

"All right then," Mr. Schlumm said, "let's get going."

Meanwhile Mr. Touren and his party were occupied with their own search for Chaya in another part of the forest. "We must find her, we must find her," he murmured continuously.

"With the help of Hashem, we will," Mr. Metzer tried to assure him.

"Our only daughter, our only child. If, God forbid, something has happened to her, I don't know what I'll do. Poor Elisheva, waiting at home full of anxiety and fear."

"Nava, describe to us exactly what happened when you all reached the clearing," Mr. Schlumm said.

Nava cast her mind back to earlier that evening. "We came to the clearing at about six-thirty," she began, "and after we put down our...backpacks, we were...assen..."

"Assigned?"

"Yes, yes, assigned to certain jobs. I was...assigned to collecting wood for our fire, and so was Chaya. After we built it, everyone danced around. I sat on the side watching and Chaya came to join me." Nava's voice grew stronger, and she found a certain comfort in describing and remembering the events.

"We both thought that everything was so beautiful, we must take pictures. But she could not find her camera. She thought that maybe she dropped it while collecting wood, so she went back to look. She will only be gone a few minutes, she said."

"Did she tell anyone else where she was going?"

"We know the answer to that one already," Mr. Mendle interjected. "Their teacher told us the whole story earlier."

"Well, I think it is imperative that we go over everything until we are familiar with every single detail," Mr. Schlumm replied. "Perhaps Miss Rimon omitted something important. People often forget important things when they're under stress. Nava, I repeat, did she tell anyone else where she was going?"

"No, no one. Only me," Nava replied sheepishly. Mr. Mendle sighed.

"Where exactly did you collect wood for the fire?" Mr. Schlumm asked.

Nava scanned the area for a few moments and then at last pointed. "Through there," she said. The five men turned to where she was pointing — a dense mass of towering trees, swaying and bending in the howling wind.

Elisheva Touren was overwrought and restless. She wandered from one room to the other, pacing up and down, gazing at the telephone, checking the clock on the wall. As she stared out the rain-streaked window at the relentless storm, she thought of her daughter alone and helpless out there. After saying some *Tehillim*, she impulsively brought out an old family photograph album and as she leafed through pictures of Chaya on happier occasions, her tears fell silently.

"I think I've found something!" Mr. Metzer cried. Mr. Touren and the rest of the group hurried over to where he was kneeling, studying something that glinted in the muddy earth. Mr. Touren bent down and frantically dug the mud away with his hands. It was Chaya's camera. "So she never even found it," he whispered.

"Hey! Look over here, quickly!" Mr. Nachshon called. Nava, her father, and the others rushed over to Mr. Nachshon, and there, on the ground, lay one of Chaya's sneakers.

"I think we must be getting close," Dr. Letchkov said.

Elisheva Touren could not bare it any longer. She picked up the telephone and dialed the Letchkovs' number. The ringing seemed endless, but at last some-one picked up the receiver at the other end.

"Hello?"

"Hello, Mrs. Letchkov? This is Elisheva Touren. I'm sorry if I woke you."

"No, no, I was awake. Is there news?"

"I haven't heard anything. That's why I called *you*. You haven't heard yet from Nava or your husband?"

"No, I'm sorry, I haven't, but I am sure they will call soon. They are probably very far from a telephone."

"Will you please call me the minute someone tele-phones you?"

"Of course, of course, but I'm sure that they will call you first."

"Thank you. I'm so sorry to have troubled you, but I am terribly worrried."

"You did not trouble me, and I can imagine what you must be going through, but try not to worry too much. *B'ezras Hashem*, they will find her tonight, and I am sure that you will hear from them soon."

Mr. Touren and the rest of his group were still in pursuit, but had all but given up any expectations of tracking down his daughter that night. Discovering Chaya's camera had really shaken him. The ever-optimistic Mr. Metzer, though, had not lost hope and kept offering words of encouragement and comfort. But nothing helped; the only comfort Mr. Touren wanted was his Chaya.

"We can't be far now," said Dr. Letchkov.

"Chaya!" Mr. Schlumm shouted. "Can you hear

me?" The others followed suit and took turns calling her name.

Nava unexpectedly began to squint and shone her flashlight in a wide arc ahead of her. She took a couple of steps forward and drew to a halt. The others stood still and watched her wordlessly. "What has she found?" Mr. Sherim whispered.

She pointed the beam before her once again and then took a few more steps forward. He heart skipped a beat, and then she let out a scream.

"Nava," Dr. Letchkov said as calmly as possible. "Nava, what is it?"

She pointed to what she had seen, trembling too much to answer. About ten meters away they could see a fallen tree — and Chaya lay trapped underneath it. Dr. Letchkov rushed to Chaya's side.

"What shall we do? Is she...breathing?" Mr. Schlumm asked, his voice strained.

"Yes, she's breathing, thank God," Dr. Letchkov replied, feeling her pulse. "She is unconscious, most likely from being hit by the tree. It is a bit difficult to determine how serious her condition is. She should not be moved by us, but the tree must be lifted off her immediately."

They all took hold of the tree and slowly and carefully attempted to ease it off Chaya. Even with the six of them straining together, they were barely able to raise the massive trunk from her still form. It was only after much stopping and starting that they succeeded at last in lifting the tree clear of Chaya and heaving it aside. When they finally completed the operation, Chaya's condition was revealed. She lay there limp and soaking wet, covered in mud and full of cuts and scratches.

"Nava and I will wait with Chaya," Dr. Letchkov said as he regained his breath. "Mr. Mendle and Mr. Schlumm, please drive to the nearest hospital and fetch help. It is better if two of you go together in this bad weather. Mr. Sherim and Mr. Nachshon, please find and alert the other groups."

"We will be as quick as possible," Mr. Mendle said as he rushed off with Mr. Schlumm.

"I think I should bring her a blanket from the car," Dr. Letchkov told Nava as he covered Chaya with his raincoat. "I don't really like to leave you, though."

"I'll be all right."

"Are you sure?"

"Yes."

"I won't be long."

He walked off into the night and returned some time later carrying a warm blanket under his arm. He covered Chaya carefully with it and then stood together with Nava, waiting.

10

"CHAYA, MY CHAYA! Where is she?" Mr. Touren cried, barely managing to hold back his tears. Nava could not tell whether they were tears of relief at finding Chaya or despair upon hearing her condition.

"She is lying over there," Dr. Letchkov told him softly. "Be careful not to touch her or move her. I am not sure how serious her injuries are."

"How is she?" Mr. Nachshon asked.

"Her condition is the same."

"Well, I've alerted all the others and they should be on their way right now. Mr. Mendle and Mr. Schlumm are still not back?"

"No. I suspect that they are having a little trouble on the roads."

Mr. Mendle and Mr. Schlumm were indeed having problems. "You know, I'm sure we passed this stretch of road before," Mr. Mendle said.

"It all looks the same in the dark," Mr. Schlumm replied. Do *you* know where we are?"

"Well, not exactly."

"I thought you told me that you knew this route."

"I thought I did, but it's a bit difficult to see where we are when it's pitch black and pouring."

"So what do you suggest I do now?"

"For a start I suggest you turn off this road: there's a fallen tree blocking the way."

It was 1:00 A.M. and still no call. What could be taking them so long? Elisheva Touren agonized. Perhaps something terrible had happened and they were all trying to pluck up the courage to telephone her. She wouldn't telephone Mrs. Letchkov again; it was far too late for that. Elisheva decided to try and get some sleep, even though she knew it would be all but impossible that night.

"What is taking them so long?" Mr. Touren despaired. "My daughter lies here with who-knows-what, and they take their time as if they were on a family outing."

"Calm down," Mr. Metzer replied. "I'm sure that they're doing their best."

"Well, their best isn't good enough!" Mr. Touren burst out. He paused abruptly, shocked at his own unfair accusation. "I'm sorry. Of course you're right. They are surely doing all they can, and I am very grateful. For a moment, I just seemed to lose my reason."

"Quite understandable," Mr. Metzer assured him. "We're all under strain."

"We can't go on — we've got two flat tires now!" Mr. Schlumm exclaimed, pulling off his round, steel-framed glasses and wiping them on his raincoat in obvious agitation.

"Well, what are we going to do? That poor girl is lying in the forest, and instead of fetching help, we're stranded here on this strange dark road," Mr. Mendle replied.

"At this very moment I think that we could do with some help ourselves."

"Then I suggest you think of a way to obtain it. If we hadn't turned up the wrong road, this would never have happened!"

"I'm sorry."

"No, I am. Please forgive me. I'm so tensed up worrying about poor Chaya that I can't seem to stop flying off the handle."

"I know, I know. I just hope and pray that she'll be all right."

"Hey! Look over there! Are those the lights of a truck? I think help may be on its way."

Mr. Mendle flashed his headlights on and off furiously while Mr. Schlumm waved his arms about trying to attract attention. At last the truck drew to a halt and the driver climbed down.

"You two look like you could use some help," he said. "Is there anything I can do?"

"Yes, yes, we need an ambulance immediately," Mr. Mendle answered quickly.

"Don't you mean a pick-up truck?"

Mr. Mendle glanced back at the car. "No, we can worry about the car later. Right now we need to summon an ambulance."

"Well, hop in. I'll take you to the nearest hospital. It's only about two miles away."

"Thank you very much."

Mr. Mendle and Mr. Schlumm hoisted themselves up into the truck's cabin. As the driver started the engine, he turned to them and asked curiously: "Why do you need an ambulance?"

"Our daughters went on a class outing today. One of the girls got lost in the woods, so we all went out to search for her. We eventually found her, trapped under a fallen tree and unconscious. We were on our way to fetch help, but when we got the two flat tires we couldn't go on."

"Poor thing — how terrible! Where did they go for their outing?"

"Tree-Glade."

"Tree-Glade? You want to take an ambulance through Tree-Glade? You'll need a rescue van, mister, not an ambulance."

Mrs. Letchkov sat in the living room next to the telephone, debating whether or not to telephone Mrs. Touren.

"No word about Chaya yet?"

"Oh, Ben-Zion! I didn't see you there. No, I haven't

eard a thing. I was just wondering whether I should all Mrs. Touren or not. Maybe she's heard."

"She's probably in bed already, and you know, ama, you should try to get some sleep as well."

"I don't know, I really don't think that I could sleep ght. And anyway, there has to be someone up in as there's a phone call."

'No problem, I can stay up."

Don't you think you should get some sleep your-elf, en-Zion?"

' m fine, Mama, but you really look tired."

" Ari asleep?"

"'s, he's been asleep for hours. Now don't worry — just o to bed. I will let you know the minute someone alls."

"O , thank you, Ben-Zion."

"I see you're without a car," the friendly rescue van driver commented. "How did you manage to get here?"

"We had a car, but got two flat tires on the way. A truckdriver stopped for us and drove us the rest of the way to the hospital," Mr. Schlumm explained.

"How long do you think it will take us to reach Tree-Glade?" Mr. Mendle asked anxiously.

"Oh, about twenty minutes, I'd say. Normally the journey is far quicker but tonight, in this rainstorm, everything has been slowed down."

"Don't you think we should send someone else out for help?" Mr. Touren asked. "Who knows what's become of them?"

"Yes, you're right." Dr. Letchkov agreed. "I was thinking the same thing myself. It is not at all good for Chaya to be out in the rain like this. It could be extremely dangerous."

"I will go," Mr. Metzer volunteered, but was cut short by the sound of approaching voices.

"Here we are at last!"

Mr. Metzer turned around quickly to see Mr. Mendle, Mr. Schlumm and a couple of paramedics hurrying toward them. "*Baruch Hashem!*" he exclaimed. "Where have you been? I was about to come out myself to fetch help."

"Where's the girl?" one of the paramedics interjected.

"Right over here," Dr. Letchkov replied, the relief in his voice evident.

"Out of the way, please, people. You have the scoop stretcher, Steve?" the paramedic asked.

"Right here, John," his partner replied.

Nava watched as the two paramedics carefully and efficiently placed Chaya on the stretcher and carried her cautiously across the slippery ground to the waiting rescue van which was parked nearby. Mr. Touren walked alongside Chaya, his shoulders bent and his face pallid with worry. Nava's father accompanied Mr. Touren. "Would you like me to come with you to the hospital?" he inquired gently.

Mr. Touren nodded. "Yes, thank you, but the rest of you, please go home. It's late, I am sure that you're all exhausted and soaked through. I am eternally grateful to you all for finding Chaya. You have done a great *mitzvah*. I will let you know how she is in the morning, *im yirtzeh Hashem*."

"Take care of yourself," Mr. Metzer called.

Mr. Touren nodded and produced a weak smile.

The men began to disperse toward their separate cars; this was not the time for small talk. Dr. Letchkov and Nava climbed into their car and followed the rescue van to the hospital.

"Nava, you are drenched and exhausted. Don't you think I should take you home first?" Dr. Letchkov asked.

"I must see how Chaya is," Nava insisted, trying to stifle a yawn.

"I think that it's still going to be quite a long while before we know anything," her father told her.

They had been waiting for almost two hours; it was now four o'clock in the morning. Upon arrival at the hospital, Nava had immediately been assigned the task of telephoning her mother to report what was happening, and then the much more difficult job of reporting to Chaya's mother. Mr. Touren couldn't tear himself away from Chaya's side.

Nava shivered even now at the recollection of it. Nava had stammered, trying to find the right words to break the news gently to Mrs. Touren.

"Nava," she burst out, "just tell me how she is."

Nava did precisely that and cringed as Mrs. Touren let out a piercing, heartrending cry. Nava was completely at a loss for words.

"I...I'm sorry, Mrs. Touren," was all she could manage before she placed the receiver down. She was still staring at it five minutes later when her father returned from the emergency room.

"How did she take it?" he asked, studying Nava's pinched face.

"Terribly."

"Of course, of course," he sighed.

A short time later Mrs. Touren arrived, pale and disheveled. "Where is Chaya?" she asked tremulously.

"She's still in the emergency room."

"I must see her! Let me see her!"

Mr. Touren came into the waiting room at that point. "Elisheva! How good to see you! The doctors are examining her now, and I think she's about to have an X ray. You will see her soon."

"But I want to see her now," she cried. "I must know that she is out of danger."

"She's in good hands, my dear, and you will be able to see her soon. We'll sit here with Nava and Dr. Letchkov in the waiting room. I'm sure it won't take too long."

Almost two hours later they were still waiting.

"What is taking so long?" Nava whispered to her father.

"I don't know. There may be several reasons. Perhaps they are waiting for the results of certain tests. Now, Nava, will you please let me drive you home? You've been up all night."

"Do you promise you'll call home as soon as you know something?"

"Yes, of course. Come on, now, I will drive you home and then come straight back. I will probably be here for the rest of the night — what's left of it."

Nava surrendered. "All right, then, I will go home."

She arrived home so drained —both emotionally and physically — that she could hardly move. She collapsed on her bed, fully clothed, and fell immediately into a deep, dreamless sleep.

11

NAVA AWOKE TO a chorus of singing birds. Sometime during the early morning hours the storm had abated, and now the sun smiled down from a cloudless, blue sky. Nava felt tranquil and happy; it was going to be a beautiful day. Suddenly she sat up with a start, as the previous day's events came flooding back to her. Chaya!

There was a gentle knock at the door.

"It's okay, I'm up," Nava called.

"Good morning, Nava," her mother said, coming into the room. "Or should I say 'good afternoon'?"

"Why? What time is it?"

"It's already past twelve. But it's good that you slept so long — you needed it, after last night. Look, you were so exhausted that you did not even change into pajamas."

Nava looked at her clothes, all crumpled and creased with traces of mud here and there. "I don't even remember what happened when I came home last night."

"Papa says you were already asleep in the car."

Nava jumped up suddenly. "Has Papa telephoned about Chaya yet?"

"Yes," her mother smiled. "She is going to be fine."

"*Baruch Hashem*! Oh, *baruch Hashem*! But tell me more — what exactly is her condition?"

"Well, she's suffering from a bad chill, overexposure, a sprained ankle, a broken arm and many cuts and bruises. Other than that, she's fine."

"Then why was she unconscious last night?"

"Papa says that it was a concussion. She is conscious now, though, and just needs rest."

"When can I go and see her?"

"Perhaps this evening. We will see what Papa says when he comes home. He is at work now, and he called and told me that Chaya might be transferred there, to his hospital, in a couple of days. The Country Hospital is in such an out-of-the-way place, and Milton Hospital is far easier to reach."

Nava fully agreed with that. She remembered that it had taken them ages to drive home the previous night — almost an hour — whereas Milton Hospital was only ten minutes away by car.

"When will she be released from the hospital?"

"No one is sure yet. Perhaps in a week or two; it depends on her condition. Oh, yes! How could I forget? I have some good news for you, Nava. A letter arrived this morning from Olga. Here it is."

Olga. A smile spread across Nava's face as she saw

the familiar handwriting on the envelope. Olga had been her best friend in the Soviet Union. She was so full of life and hope; even when things seemed gray and bleak, Olga always managed somehow to remain optimistic. It was Olga who had always cheered Nava up.

Nava remembered the day she received a picture of *Yerushalayim* from an English tourist, and had run to show it to Olga. The two of them were enchanted by its beauty and stared at it for a long time. The next day Olga appeared with a copy of Nava's picture, which she had drawn herself from memory, but in one corner she had added two small figures with faces upturned to the *Kosel Ha-Ma'aravi*. "Look, they are us," Olga declared simply. "One day we will stand together and see the beautiful city of *Yerushalayim* spread out before us."

"Will that day ever come?" Nava asked.

Olga gazed at her with a dreamy expression on her face. "Yes, very soon that day will come, and we will be together in *Yerushalayim*."

The day that Nava and her family were notified that they had finally received exit visas, Olga came to visit her. She was as ecstatic as if she herself had been given permission to leave — Nava sensed no jealousy or resentment at all. "See," she bubbled, "it is finally happening, exactly like I told you it would. Soon we will be given our visas too, and then we will be together again in *Yerushalayim*. It is starting! This is only the beginning."

The day they were to leave, Nava went to say goodbye to Olga. "I'm going to miss you terribly, Olga," Nava said, clasping her friend's hands. "I feel so sad when I think that we are leaving, and you have to stay here."

"Do not worry, my friend," Olga assured her. "Soon we will be reunited in Israel."

Nava reached into her pocket and drew out the picture of *Yerushalayim* which Olga had copied. "Take this and keep it until we meet again, until the two of us are in *Yerushalayim* together as you drew us here," she whispered, hugging her dear friend, "when I will be 'Nava' and you will be 'Osnat.'"

Nava opened her letter eagerly and read:

> Dearest Nadja,
> How are you? How are you settling down in England? Have you made a lot of new friends? Are you learning English quickly? What is England like? Here, things remain much the same. School is boring and last week we had a few tests but they were not too bad. I hope to receive my results this week.
> Mother has managed to find a job at last; it is a secretarial position in a hospital. She is very pleased with it, and the work is interesting.
> I have decided to learn a foreign language because it is sure to help me in the future. Languages are always useful, don't you think?
> Please don't forget me.
>
> With love,
> Olga.

Nava reread the letter a few times, scrutinizing it for secret meanings between the lines, for things that couldn't be written. The foreign language which Olga was referring to must be *Ivrit*, Nava decided. Ever-idealistic Olga, Nava thought, always looking at the bright side of things and preparing for the future. Nava brought out a photograph of the two of them together, which she always kept in the drawer of her bedside table along with the precious picture of *Yerushalayim* that she had received from the tourist. The photograph had been taken on Nava's twelfth birthday — her *Bas Mitzvah* — and showed the two friends standing together with their arms around each other. Nava was wearing a brand new dress which her mother had made especially for her birthday, her straight, raven hair tied back with a matching blue ribbon. Olga wore a green dress, and her soft curls, the color of ripe corn, fell gently about her face. As Nava gazed at the photograph, two pairs of twinkling brown eyes looked back at her, shining with joy and hope. "Olga," she murmured, taking one last look at the picture, and then placed it back in the drawer.

Nava walked along the hospital corridor with her father, sensing the familiar antiseptic, medicinal odor that all hospitals seem to have. She was apprehensive about seeing Chaya: In what condition would she find her, and how would Chaya react toward her?

"She's in here," Dr. Letchkov said, pointing at a door and steering Nava into the room.

Chaya sat propped up in bed, surrounded by piles of books. Nava took it all in: the bandaged foot, the arm in a cast, and the dark circles around Chaya's eyes, which were made all the darker by her pale, wan face.

When Chaya saw Nava, her face brightened instantly. "Nava! It's so good to see you. I've been bored stiff here today!"

"Chaya, I...I am sorry," Nava stammered, unable to meet her eyes.

"Sorry? What on earth for?"

"For letting you go off like that...for allowing this ...terrible thing to happen to you."

"I'm the one who should be saying 'I'm sorry'! I heard how bad you were feeling last night, and I feel terrible for all the trouble and anguish I caused. It was stupid of me to run off like that without telling Miss Rimon or Miss Tovim first."

Relief flooded Nava when she heard Chaya's words. She didn't blame her after all! For a moment she stood there mutely, not knowing what to say, and then she found her voice. "Did you find your camera?"

"No! What happened was that I became utterly lost, and couldn't even find the way back, let alone my camera. My Dad found it, though, and brought it to me this morning and you know what? It has survived being dropped, soaked and buried in mud."

"Oh, Chaya, was it really horrible being in the forest alone?"

"It was awful! While there was still light even though I felt rather scared it was not too bad, because I could still see where I was going and I kept thinking that I would surely find the way. But once it got dark and the storm began, I could only see when the lightning flashed. That's how I sprained my ankle. I tripped on something that I didn't see, and then I had to crawl across the wet, muddy ground because it was too painful to walk. I actually saw the tree falling toward me, but because of my leg I couldn't get out of the way in time." Chaya shuddered a moment at the memory and then went on. "The doctors told me that I was very lucky — my injuries could have been a lot more serious than a concussion and a broken arm. I don't really like to think about that, though. I think that I am still a bit shaken over it."

"Are you in great pain, Chaya?"

"It's not too bad. And," she added with her characteristic cheerfulness, "at least it was my left arm that was broken, and not my right; otherwise I wouldn't have been able to write for weeks and it's boring enough here as it is!" Chaya stopped chattering and looked steadily into Nava's eyes. "Nava, I don't know how to thank you for getting everyone to look for me last night and for coming back yourself. I'm so sorry for causing so much trouble."

"It was not trouble," Nava murmured, fighting rising tears, "and I was so relieved to find you. Now tell me, Chaya, how is your mother?"

"She's fine, but very tired after the ordeal. Was she very upset last night?"

"Well…I would say yes…a little." Nava suddenly became conscious of someone else in the room, and turned around to see a nurse standing in the doorway.

"Excuse me," the nurse said in a brisk but friendly tone, "I'm afraid you will have to leave now. The doctor is here to see Chaya."

"*Refuah shelemah*, Chaya," Nava told her friend, rising to leave. "I will try to come again tomorrow." She waved to Chaya before heading back down the corridor to where her father was waiting for her. "Thank you, Hashem," she whispered, "for making everything turn out all right."

12

NAVA, DID YOU HEAR?" Sharon asked, excited. "Chaya was discharged from the hospital yesterday!"

"Yes, I know. She called me last night. I am so happy that she came home in time for *Shavuos*."

"Are you going to be visiting her soon?"

"Yes — I will probably go tomorrow."

"Do you mind if I come with you?"

"Not at all. I will stop by for you, since your house is on the way."

The following afternoon, the two girls paid Chaya a visit. They found her as cheerful as usual and delighted to be home. Her sprained ankle had healed and her arm was mending well. Nava hoped now that with time, they would all be able to put the horrible incident at Tree-Glade behind them.

It was *erev Shavuos* and Batsheva High School seemed to reverberate with preparations for the short holiday break. Many of the teachers handed back marked homework and tests, while others rushed around ushering everyone into the hall for the special *Shavuos* assembly.

School finished very early that day, and Nava arrived home to find her mother in the kitchen engaged in the last few preparations.

"Hello, Nava!" she called. "Come, I have something to show you."

"Hello, Mama! What's up?"

Mrs. Letchkov smiled. Her daughter sounded very English to her ears. "Nothing is 'up.' I just want to show you this cheesecake. Mrs. Ravman gave me the recipe this morning. What do you think?"

The cheesecake looked delicious: golden and crunchy on the top, with a delicate, soft cheese filling.

"Mama, it looks and smells heavenly."

Mrs. Letchkov beamed with pleasure and pride, gratified at her daughter's approval. Now that they were free to observe all the holidays to the fullest, she wanted to do everything just right, down to the last detail.

"Can I have a taste, please?" Nava asked.

"Sorry, but no. I don't want you eating it all up now. You can have some tonight for dessert."

"I can't wait! Are Ben-Zion and Ari home yet?"

"No, they finish a little later than you today."

"And Tikva?"

"She's upstairs playing with her toys."

Nava's little sister was called *Tikva* — hope — because Tikva's difficult birth had brought hope to her parents. If Tikva — their miracle baby — could be born, the Letchkovs felt that anything was possible, even permission to leave the Soviet Union. And sure enough, three years later they received their exit visas.

As Nava got dressed for the holiday, her thoughts went back to the shopping trip with her mother and Tikva, when they had bought beautiful new dresses for *Shavuos*. Nava had carried her purchase out of the shop feeling very pleased with herself — she was now the proud owner of a beautiful, white cotton dress with a matching jacket. It was the first new item of clothing she had bought in a long time. Tikva walked grandly at her sister's side carrying her bag, which held a new sailor dress. Nava reveled in the luxury of being able to buy any item of clothing she wished, without having to worry about being eyed by suspicious and jealous neighbors.

"I'm home!" Dr. Letchkov called. "Would someone mind helping me with all of these?" The Letchkov family emerged from all corners of the house to see what Dr. Letchkov's burden was, and they gazed in rapture when they saw it. He stood in the hall, smiling broadly, bearing bunches upon bunches of brightly colored flowers.

"This is our first real *Shavuos*," he declared, "so I decided that we will celebrate properly! Do we have enough vases?"

"I'm sure that we can find enough," Mrs. Letchkov murmured in reply, sudden tears filling her eyes.

Vases and jars were hurriedly fetched, and flowers cut and arranged. Within no time, the whole house was filled with a riot of color and had taken on the appearance of a florist's shop: daffodils, narcissus, roses, tulips, lily of the valley, lavender and carnations all graced their household with a true *Shavuos* spirit.

"And do you know what, Chana?" Dr. Letchkov announced to his wife, smiling as if he had a delightful secret to reveal. "In *shul* there will be Torah learning all night tonight."

"Will you be going?" she asked.

"Of course! Can you imagine it — being able to learn Torah openly, the whole night, without having to worry about the K.G.B.!"

The day after *Shavuos*, as was their family custom after a *Yom Tov* or Shabbos, they took all the mail that had accumulated over the holiday and spread it out on the dining room table to read. Mrs. Letchkov opened the first letter and her face immediately fell.

"What is it? What has happened? Who is it from?" Everyone asked anxiously.

Mrs. Letchkov's face was ashen. "It is from Grandmother."

13

NAVA WALKED INTO CLASS with a distant and pained expression on her face, her usually sparkling eyes dull and lifeless.

"Hi, Nava! Aren't you glad to see me back?" Chaya called.

"Yes, I am very glad, Chaya," she answered flatly. "It is good that you are back." The words were empty, the voice lacked enthusiasm and there was no accompanying smile.

"Nava?" The bell rang for the start of the first lesson. "Nava, I must go to art class now, but I'll speak to you during the break. All right?"

Nava nodded mechanically and watched her friend race off toward the art room before she herself went to sewing class, a lesson which she detested profoundly.

In art class, while attempting to produce a still-life charcoal drawing of fruit tumbling out of a shopping bag, Chaya spoke to Rachel and Naama about Nava.

"I can't imagine what's troubling her," Chaya

began. "When I saw her over *Yom Tov* she seemed fine, and now she suddenly seems depressed and unhappy."

"Did you try asking her about it?" Rachel asked her.

"No, I haven't had the chance. I told her that I would speak to her during our break."

"Okay, but I don't think that we should pry too much," Naama added. "It may be something private."

"Well," Rachel replied, "if she doesn't want to tell us, she doesn't have to, but I think we should at least ask her what's wrong to show her that we care."

"Naama!" Mrs. Trainer's call put a quick end to the girls' hurried conference. "Can I see what you have accomplished this lesson, please?" Naama slowly made her way to the front of the class, where Mrs. Trainer sat at her desk. "M-m-m, your perspective is quite good, but where are the shadows? And you've forgotten to fore-shorten the bag. Remember, it must be wider in the front and get gradually narrower the closer it gets to the back. Even though the bag is long, you must try not to draw it as you know that it is, but rather as you see it. Otherwise the proportion will be all wrong."

"Yes, Mrs. Trainer."

"And if you had not talked so much, you would have remembered that by yourself."

"Yes, Mrs. Trainer."

"Now go and sit down, and do more drawing and less talking."

"Nava, what have you done?" Nava jerked her head up, confused, and saw Mrs. Johnson standing over her looking aghast.

"Wh…what do you mean?" Nava mumbled.

"Your hemming! It's all wrong! Your stitches are too small and tight, and besides that, you haven't spaced them evenly at all."

"I am sorry."

"Rip it all out and start again. If you concentrate, this time you will do it properly."

During the recess break, Chaya, Rachel and Naama found Nava wandering aimlessly around the spacious grounds that surrounded the school.

"Do you want to talk?" Chaya asked her. Nava shrugged her shoulders.

"Something is wrong, very wrong — we can see that. Is it really serious?" Rachel asked.

"Yes," Nava replied. "It is very serious."

"Perhaps we could help," Naama suggested gently.

"I want very much to tell you of it because I know this will make me feel better, but I do not think that anything can be done this time."

"Well, tell us," Rachel said matter-of-factly, "and we will see what we can do."

Nava was silent for a moment and then drew a shaky breath. "Over *Yom Tov* my mother received a letter from my grandmother in the Soviet Union."

"Your grandmother? I didn't know…"

"Rachel, let Nava talk," Naama scolded.

"She wrote that the doctors told her that she must have operations on both her eyes," Nava continued in a small, tense voice. "My grandmother, though, refuses to do it unless my father, her son-in-law, either performs the operation or is there. You see, she is very frightened but she trusts my father. She says that she would feel safe if he were there. But my father, of course, cannot go back there, and my grandmother cannot get out of the Soviet Union: she did not get permission to leave like we did. If she does not have the operations soon, she may become blind."

"Oh, Nava! That's really terrible. I'm sorry. I don't know what to say," Rachel blurted awkwardly. "How come you've never told us about her before?"

"This may be hard for you to understand," Nava began, a flush rising on her pale cheeks, "but I feel ...guilty. We were allowed to leave, but she was not. We left her behind. She is an old woman and has been praying to leave for years, far longer than we. But we were allowed out and she is still there. The day we heard that we had been given permission to leave, we were at first overjoyed, but then we learned that my grandmother had not gotten permission. We decided that we would not leave. How could we go and let her stay all alone in the Soviet Union?

"But my grandmother insisted that we must leave, because, she said, if we did not go when we could, we may never have a second chance. She finally convinced us that if we were living in England or Israel, there would be a greater chance that the authorities would let her go, because she could then say that she wants to join her family living outside of Russia. But so far, nothing has changed. My grandmother has applied now again, telling them about her medical condition but I think that she has been refused again."

Chaya shook her head. "There must be *something* that we can do."

"I do not think so," Nava replied sadly. The bell rang, signaling the end of the recess break.

"I'll think of something," Chaya said, before they all went back.

There must be a way, Chaya thought during English class. We must help somehow! While everyone else sat writing a timed essay, Chaya sat with her pen poised in mid-air, thinking. At last a plan began to emerge in her mind. Yes! She had formulated a brillant plan to help Nava's grandmother leave Russia. With a huge sense of relief, she began to work it out in greater detail.

"Chaya!" Mrs. Parker rapped.

Chaya jumped. "Uh, yes, Mrs. Parker?"

"Please get on with your work!"

"Yes, Mrs. Parker." How would she ever wait until the next break?

Ten minutes before the end of the lesson, Chaya finished her essay and did not know how she was going to occupy herself for the next ten, endless minutes. Agitated, she began to methodically disassemble all her pens. Five minutes to go! Chaya returned her pens to their original state. Two minutes to go! Mrs. Parker said, "Pens down," and began to collect the papers. One minute to go! Chaya began to count the seconds until the end of the lesson. Time for the bell to ring, but it did not.

"Come on, come on," Chaya whispered urgently. Ten seconds late: Chaya felt like pounding on her desk.

There was a loud, steady ring — the bell! Chaya charged out of the classroom faster than the speed of light. In the hall, she waited for everyone to follow and practically dragged Nava through the classroom door.

"What's up?" Shira asked. "What's with this sudden haste?"

"I have an idea. Come out with me to the playground."

"Well, what's your idea?" Rachel asked, settling herself comfortably on a patch of grass.

Nava regarded her silently, a faint flicker — could it be hope? — in her brown eyes.

"I've been thinking a great deal about what you told us this morning," Chaya began, "and I've thought of a way to help your grandmother because — first and foremost — you are my friend and I feel your pain. But I also want to help you because of the way you helped me when I was lost in Tree-Glade — something I'm eternally grateful to you for."

Chaya looked around at her friends, her excited glance encompassing them all. "The first thing we will do is start to circulate a petition which everyone in school will sign, and then we will hand it in to the Soviet Embassy. Secondly, we will all write letters of protest to the Soviet government."

"That is a brilliant idea!" Naama exclaimed.

"It's definitely worth a try," Rachel agreed.

"You…would…do all this for me?" Nava asked in wonder.

"You're our friend," Chaya replied simply. "We'll do anything we can to help you."

14

AS NAVA LEFT SCHOOL that day, she allowed herself to dare to think that perhaps…perhaps there was still a chance for her grandmother — and even if the plan did not work, it would at least be some comfort to know that they had tried everything possible.

As she struggled to fall asleep that night, the day's events replayed themselves in Nava's mind. Chaya is such a good friend, she thought; she's always willing to help me, and she's thankful for the little I did for her when she was lost in Tree-Glade. She says that she is eternally grateful to me for what I did for her, but it is really I who must be forever indebted to her, for befriending me and giving me hope.

Hope. In that way Chaya reminded her of Olga. She too would have come up with some master plan, when everyone else was convinced that the situation was impossible. Just like Olga, Nava mused, and drifted into a peaceful sleep.

When Nava reached school the next day, Chaya was waiting for her at the gate with clipboard in hand.

"Nava," she announced, "I have the petition here. Rachel, Naama and Sharon also have copies and are already going around the school with them. Would you like to put your signature down first?"

"Oh, Chaya," Nava exclaimed, "you're wonderful!" And she proudly signed her name.

"This lunch break we'll talk about the letter-writing campaign. I think Rachel is organizing that."

"Is there anything *I* can do?" Nava asked.

"No," replied Chaya resolutely. "You have enough to worry about. We'll take care of everything."

"Thank you," murmured Nava softly.

"What for?"

"For all that you are doing for me. It means so much to have caring friends like you."

"But friends are supposed to share their burdens as well as their joys, and help each other in time of need. If they can't do that, what sort of people are they? Have you ever heard of the saying: 'One good turn deserves another'? It means that if someone does something to help you, then that person deserves your help in return."

"That is a nice saying," Nava said thoughtfully. And then, shyly, she added, "You know, Chaya, this is what we learned in *Chumash* class last week. Avimelech said to Avraham, 'According to the kindness that I have done to you, you shall do to me.'"

"Nava," Chaya grinned, "you're only here a short while and you remember more *Chumash* than I do!"

Nava neatly folded up her letter, placed it in the envelope and added it to the fast-growing pile.

"We already have over fifty letters," Rachel informed her.

"It was a brilliant idea," Nava replied.

"And do you know how many signatures we have on the petition? Over two hundred — that's over half the school. Everyone is signing — all the pupils, the teachers, and even the janitor and cleaning staff."

"Everybody in the school has written a letter, everybody!" Rachel informed Nava excitedly while walking home from school the following week.

"And everyone has signed the petition!" Chaya added.

"This is amazing! Unbelievable!" Nava exclaimed.

"And I have another idea," Sharon said. "I'm going to get my brother to take around a petition at his school, and Naama said that she'll get her brother to organize the protest letters."

"That will be…"

"And I'll go around with the petition to everyone in the neighborhood," Rachel interrupted.

"No one could have better friends than you," Nava said fervently, her eyes filling with tears of gratitude.

It was dark and strangely cold for a night in early June. Nava shivered, yet was drawn to the front door. She went out into the garden, barefoot, not even bothering to put on shoes or a sweater. Outside, she was unable to see anything through the thick swirling mists, and the howling wind terrified her. She heard the door slam shut behind her and Nava realized that she was locked out of the house. In panic she ran back, only to find that she could no longer even see her house; it was completely shrouded in cold, damp mist. Nava did not know where to turn, and she wandered around with her hands outstretched before her, desperately trying to find her house.

Then the mist began to clear.

The first thing she noticed was the glittering white ground beneath her. Snow! She was walking on snow! How odd, Nava thought — snow in June! Her bare feet were numb with cold and she stood still, unable to walk further. She watched as the haze gave way to reveal a strange scene in front of her: Rachel, Chaya, Naama and Sharon were walking toward her with clipboards in their hands. They waved and tried to show her how many signatures they had collected on their petitions but then stopped, as if in fright, and began to back away. They turned around and walked into…her apartment block! It was then that it dawned on Nava where she was. She was in Moscow! In the winter!

"Wait!" Nava called to her friends. "Wait for me!" She ran after them but a man blocked the doorway. A K.G.B. agent, he looked down at her with a sneer. "Please," Nava pleaded, "my friends are inside. Would you be so kind as to let me pass?"

The man laughed harshly. "That is impossible; they are being held under guard until it is time to take them away."

Nava grew tense. "Why are they being held under guard? Where are you taking them?"

"They are going to be taken to Siberia for a lifetime of hard labor, as punishment for trying to have your grandmother released. Your grandmother is already in Siberia."

"No!" Nava screamed.

"Yes," the man replied. "And as for you, I am going to be very fair. I will give you a thirty-second lead. Run, and if you escape you may go home. However, if I catch you, you will join your grandmother and your dear friends in Siberia." The man gave a cruel laugh.

Terrified, Nava began to run, but her feet were so numb that she couldn't feel them. Though she was moving her legs, still she remained in the same place — running, always running, getting nowhere. Suddenly the agent caught up with her and Nava let out a blood-curdling scream.

"Nava!"

Nava trembled and gasped for breath. "No!" she cried. "Please, no!"

"Nava, wake up!"

Nava opened her eyes to find her mother standing over her, her eyes filled with concern. "What a bad dream you were having, Nava. Are you all right now?"

Nava looked around her room. Everything was as usual. She was back in her bed and all was calm and quiet.

"What time is it, Mama?" she asked shakily.

"Almost seven," her mother replied. "You had better start getting ready for school — otherwise you'll be late."

Nava recited *Modeh Ani*, washed her hands and took a few deep breaths to calm herself. It was only a dream, she told herself, and went to dress.

Nava sat studying the pages of signatures that were spread out in front of her.

"There are over a thousand here," Naama informed her. "I'm going to send it off by registered mail as soon as I get home, and it should reach the Soviet Embassy tomorrow, or by Monday at the latest."

"All the letters from school have already been mailed," Rachel said.

"And so have the letters from David Hamelech Boys' High School," Sharon added.

"I do not know what I would do without you…" Nava began.

"And on Monday we carry out our Plan Number Two," Chaya interrupted.

"What is that?"

"We telephone the Soviet Embassy, and then we leak the whole story to the press."

On Monday, one hundred calls were made to the Soviet Embassy by the girls of Form Three, and the story was leaked to most of the major national papers. On Tuesday, Chaya greeted Nava with a small pile of newspapers: the story had not made the front pages, but it appeared with prominent headlines farther back.

"Look at this, Nava: HIGH SCHOOL PLEA FOR GRANDMOTHER'S RELEASE."

"And this one," Rachel cried: "LET MY GRAND-MOTHER GO!"

"I cannot believe it," Nava said. "They actually printed our story. I did not think they would — I could not imagine such a thing."

"Now," Chaya announced, "it is time to start Plan Number Three — the most important part of our operation: Rachel, will you organize a meeting for the whole school at the end of the day?"

"No problem," Rachel replied matter-of-factly.

Teachers and pupils alike filed into the auditorium. Chaya stood on the stage waiting with a *sefer Tehillim* in hand. Once everyone was present, she looked around at all the expectant faces and began to speak: "I don't know if all of you are aware of why we are gathered here, but I'm sure you all know of the sad plight of Nava's grandmother and how we are trying to help get her out of Russia.

"But letters and petitions are not enough in themselves." Chaya paused and took a deep breath. "The Soviet authorities have hardened their hearts just as Pharaoh hardened his. Let us pray to Hashem to soften the Russian Pharaohs' hearts and release Nava's grandmother. We want to enlist your help in reciting *Tehillim* together at the end of each school day."

Suddenly, one Sixth Former at the back raised her hand. "May I suggest we go one step further?"

"Of course," Chaya replied.

"Besides saying *Tehillim* together every day before

we leave school, we should organize a chain so that throughout the entire day there is always at least one person saying *Tehillim*."

The idea met with an enthusiastic response. *Tehillim* were said, and before the assembly broke up, plans had been set in motion to organize the whole undertaking. From that day on, the entire staff and student body — like one big united family — took part in reciting *Tehillim* daily.

15

NAVA WALKED THROUGH the school gates crestfallen and distraught.

"Nava!" Sharon called from their classroom window when she saw her walking up the path. "Today I want to tell you about Plan Number Four."

"There is no need for Plan Number Four," Nava murmured, so softly that Sharon thought at first she was talking to herself.

"What?"

"It's no use — please forget it."

"Nava, I don't understand you," Naama confronted her sullen friend during the first recess break. "Before, you were so enthusiastic about our plans, and now you seem angry and tell us to forget the whole thing. Why?"

"Naama, I…I'm sorry if I sound angry, because I am not. Well, I am — but certainly not with any of you. It's just that…"

"That what? What's wrong?"

"Last week a friend of ours went to the Soviet

Union," Nava began haltingly, "and he told us that he would be sure to visit my grandmother to see how she was. Yesterday morning he telephoned us from the Vienna airport, on his way back to England, and told us..." Here Nava paused and drew another breath. "He told us that when he went to visit my grandmother, *she was not there*."

"Oh, no!" Naama whispered.

"He came back a second time, but again she was not there. He knocked on the door of a neighbor — an elderly lady who does not speak much English — and when he asked her where my grandmother was, she just said, 'Gone.'"

"Gone?" echoed Sharon.

"Yes...gone. He asked if she had left her apartment, and the lady replied, 'Yes, left, everything gone.' Then he asked her *where* she had gone. She started to say something, he told us, but then simply shrugged her shoulders and kept silent. Naama, she has disappeared!"

"Is there nothing you can do?" Sharon cried.

"We tried to telephone the Soviet Embassy yesterday to see if they could tell us anything, but when they heard who we were asking about, they told us they could not help us and put the phone down. They are so fed up with calls about my grandmother."

"But what could have happened to her?"

"I don't know. I am scared to even think about it. All I know is that she has disappeared, and I don't know where she is."

"Nava!" Chaya called excitedly, as she and Rachel

hurried over to the group. "Has Sharon told you about our next plan yet?"

Chaya's words were met with a deep silence.

"Chaya, I must speak to you and Rachel for a moment," Sharon said. "Nava, do you mind if I tell Chaya and Rachel?"

"No, of course not. You are all my friends."

"What's wrong?" Chaya asked.

"I'll explain everything." Sharon replied.

Sharon told Chaya and Rachel the whole story, leaving them dumbfounded and confused. Tears of anger and pain welled up in their eyes, and then all five of them sat down on the grass and wept quietly together.

The bell rang for the start of morning lessons, and slowly and miserably the girls made their way to class. They drifted through the lessons, hardly paying attention to what was being taught. At last, in *Chumash* class, a fed-up Miss Tovim asked them why they were not listening to the lesson. When Rachel told the teacher the reason, she too was upset.

"Sometimes, we don't understand why bad things happen," Miss Tovim said gently, "and we're upset and confused. But if we remember to always put our trust in Hashem, then we realize that in the end — whether or not the end turns out to be the way we wanted — everything is for the best, and Hashem is the only true Judge."

"But it is so hard sometimes," Nava said.

"I know. It is very hard, Nava, but Hashem is the only true source of help, so we must place our trust in Him and pray."

"Do you think it would help, even now, to say *Tehillim?*"

"Of course. *Tefillah* always helps, and even if it does not help us here and now, it will not be wasted; it will help someone, somewhere else."

For the rest of the lesson they poured out their hearts to Hashem, reciting the *Tehillim* with more fervor than ever before. Nava tried to push out of her mind the terrifying memory of the nightmare she'd had about her grandmother and all her friends being sent to Siberia. Was that what had really happened to her grandmother? No! It has not happened, and it will not happen, she told herself firmly. But even so, she was afraid.

That evening, Nava sat with her family over dinner, and they were all unusually quiet. Her father did not relate his usual humorous stories about work, and her mother didn't tell them about whom she had met out shopping and what she had done all day. Ben-Zion and Ari were not busy reporting all the incidents that had happened that day in school. Even little Tikva, who usually chattered away happily about anything and everything, was silent.

When dinner was over they sat in the living room, still locked in their silent despair. Nava didn't feel like doing her homework, and she couldn't bring herself to play any of the family's favorite pieces on their old, badly tuned piano, as she sometimes did. Instead, she sat on the sofa and fidgeted with the fringes on the armrest; her brothers stared at nothing in particular; her father attempted to read a newspaper, but was unable to absorb the meaning of the black print in front of him. Tikva, realizing that something was seriously wrong, played with her blocks quietly on the floor. Nava's mother sat in an armchair in the corner, unmoving, deep in thought.

The sudden ring of the doorbell jolted them all back into reality. Nava slowly stood up. "I'll answer it," she said.

She went to the door, looked through the peephole and gave a short, shocked gasp before swiftly opening it.

There on the porch stood her grandmother, smiling, with a bulging suitcase in each hand. Facing her, Nava stood mesmerized and speechless.

"Grandmother? *Babushka?*" she whispered in Russian.

"Hello, my Nadja," her grandmother replied.

"*Babushka!*" Nava shrieked, throwing her arms around the woman and hugging her tightly. "Is it really you?"

Her grandmother laughed her wonderful, familiar laugh. "Well, of course! Who should it be?"

"Nava, who is at the door?" her mother called.

Nava did not reply; she could not find her voice.

"Nava!" her mother called again.

Nava tried to answer, but when she opened her mouth, no sound came. She didn't know whether to laugh or cry, call her mother or hug and kiss her grandmother some more. Her mind reeled with a thousand questions, but all she could do was stand there, mute, eyes beginning to fill with tears.

The rest of the family slowly came to the door, one my one, and they too were dumbstruck.

"Mama?" Mrs. Letchkov stammered.

"Yes, yes, it is really me. Why are you all acting as i you had just seen a ghost?"

"Because...because," Nava's mother embraced th grandmother, and then held her at arm's length an stared at her, wide-eyed with wonder.

"Perhaps we had all better sit down," Nava's grand mother suggested as she strode happily into the house followed by six zombies. Leaving her suitcases in th hall, she settled herself down in the living room an looked expectantly at the rest of the stunned family.

"Now then," she laughed, "are you happy to se me?"

Mrs. Letchkov found her voice at last. "Oh, Mama, she cried, her tears and laughter mingling. "Listen, an I'll explain everything. David Shern was in Moscow las week and he promised us that while he was there, h would visit you. Yesterday he telephoned us from th Vienna airport and said that when he went to see you you were not there. He knocked on a neighbor's door — old Mrs. Chelinsky, I think — and she said that you wer gone, that your flat was empty, and she didn't know where you were. We thought you had...disappeared and we were frantic with worry."

Nava's grandmother wiped her eyes. "No, I hadn' disappeared, *baruch Hashem*. I had only 'disappeared from Russia, and I was on my way to England, that's al As for Mrs. Chelinsky, I must have told her a doze times that I was leaving for England. But every time I le my flat, she would come out of hers and say to me: 'Mrs Jakovsky, where did you say you were going?' Really She is enough to drive anyone crazy. But they say he son is in the K.G.B., you know, so perhaps all that forgetfulness was simply an act she put on to see what she could find out. Who knows?"

She looked around at her family, and her cheerful banter faltered for a moment as her eyes filled with tears again. "I was so hoping that you would be at the airport to meet me. My eyes are so bad that I was nervous about finding your house by myself, and my English is worse than my eyes!"

"But how were we to know that you were coming?"

"I realize now that you didn't get the letter I sent, telling you that I had received permission to leave, when I would be coming, and on what flight. But I'm not surprised that the letter never arrived."

"But Mama, why didn't you telephone us from the airport?"

"I didn't have your phone number."

"But we sent it to you in our very first letter."

"Ah, but I never got the letter. In fact, I have only received one letter from you since you arrived in England."

"We must have sent you at least five!"

"I've also sent you about four or five. Our letters must have been blocked by the authorities."

"Yes, I am sure of that," Dr. Letchkov said. "But, *baruch Hashem*, we are all together now and our nightmare has ended."

"Yes, *baruch Hashem*, we are together and we are free," Mrs. Jakovsky murmured. "But there are still so many left."

"Yes, and we must never forget it," Mrs. Letchkov

added gravely. "Never."

Over cups of hot tea and slices of Mrs. Letchkov's delicious cake, the family talked of everything that had happened since their arrival in England. Mrs. Jakovsky turned to Dr. Letchkov. "How is your work, Chaim?"

"It's going very well," Dr. Letchkov replied. "It is good to be practicing medicine again." He sighed heavily, unable to continue for a moment. "It was so difficult being barred from doing my life's work after we had applied for permission to leave." He smiled at his mother-in-law. "And tomorrow I will try to schedule your eye operations."

Nava rushed into the classroom the next morning, unable to contain her excitement; but before she even had a chance to share her good news, Rachel came over to inquire how she was feeling.

"I feel great!" Nava cried. "I am so happy and full of energy that I could burst. You will…"

"But Nava, aren't you worried about your grandmother anymore?"

"Well, you see —"

"Nava, why the high spirits suddenly?" Chaya asked.

"You will not believe this. I hardly believe it myself! Listen: my grandmother just appeared at our door yesterday evening! It seems that the Soviet authorities finally gave her permission to leave. I wanted to phone you, but when I noticed the hour, it was too late to call," Nava related breathlessly.

"That is staggering!" Rachel exclaimed.

"I am so happy for you," Chaya cried, hugging Nava warmly.

As word spread quickly, the whole class became giddy with excitement and joy.

The scene reminded Nava of the day when they had found out about the *Lag Ba-Omer* outing to Tree-Glade. Little did they know then what was to happen on that trip, she mused. Recalling everything that had happened since then, Nava felt great pleasure and deep gratitude at having friends who could be so happy for another's good fortune, friends who cared so much that they were always prepared to help one another.

And their *Tehillim* campaign had brought results, Nava marveled. She wondered at what point the authorities had decided to let her grandmother out of the Soviet Union. But that was something she would never know.

16

FINAL EXAM TIME had arrived.

"I am so very nervous," Nava confided to Sharon. "I'm sure I won't be able to pay attention to the geography exam today. All I can think about is my grandmother's operation." She sighed, and then added, "Anyway, even at the best of times, I don't do well on tests."

"Don't worry," Sharon reassured her, "you'll do fine. Everyone is always nervous at the beginning of exams, but once you've taken the first one, you'll be all right."

"I hope you're right. I keep imagining how I will walk into the classroom, see the exam paper and not be able to answer a single question on it."

"I often think that too, but it never turns out to be quite as bad as all that. By the way, when exactly is your grandmother having her operation?"

"Sometime this afternoon. She is going to be admitted to the hospital at about nine-thirty this morning."

"Is she anxious about it?"

"A little, but she won't admit it. Of course, she has complete confidence in my father, but it's still frightening."

"All right, girls! Are you ready?" Miss Rimon's voice broke into their conversation.

"Yes," everyone from Form Three replied.

"Well, this is it," Sharon whispered. "Good luck, Nava, and try not to worry."

"Thank you, Sharon, and good luck to you too."

Nava sat down at her desk and began to sort out her equipment. Her heart almost skipped a beat when she took out her pens: her cartridge pen was empty and her ballpoint pen had ceased to work. She tried to keep calm and think straight, but she was petrified that she would not be able to write her examination because she had no pen, and would therefore fail the course. She was sure that her teacher would refuse to give her a pen, since it was Nava's own fault: she should have been more careful to check her supplies before walking into the exam room in the first place. At least, that's what would happen back in Russia, she thought. Frantically, Nava turned her schoolbag over onto her desk and breathed a huge sigh of relief when five cartridges flew out.

Miss Rimon began to hand out the examinations, placing each one face down. Nava was horrified as she realized that they had a whole booklet to answer in just one-and-a-half hours.

"Answers should be written in the booklet itself, but extra paper will be provided if needed," Miss Rimon announced. "Please turn your papers over now, write your name on the front page, but do nothing else."

Nava did as instructed and waited.

"The time is now nine o'clock, and you have one-and-a-half hours to complete the test. You may begin."

A rustling of paper was heard as everyone opened her exam booklet in unison. Relax and keep calm — this is only a test, Nava told herself. She scanned the questions quickly and suddenly felt her mind go blank. She could not recall a thing!

Nava took a deep breath and tried again. She studied the first question, rereading it slowly and carefully: *What is the capital of China?* She paused to think. What indeed was the capital of China? Nava remembered learning about it, but just couldn't call it to mind. Peking! That was it! Nava hurriedly wrote the answer down and began to relax.

Mrs. Jakovsky sat in the back seat of the taxi, nervously clutching her small suitcase and staring straight ahead.

"Are you all right, Mama?" Mrs. Letchkov asked.

"Of course I am all right," she answered in rapid Russian. "Why should I not be all right?"

"I thought that you looked a little worried, that's all."

"I have been through worse things in my life, believe me, and I've managed."

"I know, Mama, but if you are apprehensive, you needn't be. It's a very routine operation."

Chana Letchkov was not at all convinced that her

mother was fine; she could see that her hands were trembling and her lips were pursed tightly. As much as she could reassure her mother that the operation was a routine one, she could not promise her that it would be a success. Dr. Letchkov was not even sure himself whether the outcome would be successful, for the surgery should really have been performed earlier and the chances of success were greatly reduced now. Chana hoped that it was not too late to save her mother's sight, and she offered a fervent, silent prayer to Hashem.

"I am not worried," Mrs. Jakovsky repeated, shakily. "But it will be fine won't it, Chana? My vision will really stop deteriorating and the damage that's there already will be corrected? I cannot wait to see well again," she whispered.

"Mama, it will not help to worry. Just put your trust in Hashem."

Mrs. Jakovsky smiled a smile of great inner strength. "My trust is always with Hashem," she replied. "I am in His hands."

The taxi maneuvered into a parking space and then drew to a halt. "Here we are ladies," the driver announced. Mrs. Jakovsky gazed up at the tall, forbidding building and shuddered inwardly.

"Pens down," Miss Rimon announced. Pens clattered down onto desks, and papers were rustled again as Miss Rimon and the geography teacher stood up and began to collect all the tests. The girls sat tensely on the edge of their seats, swiftly stuffing all their paraphernalia into their schoolbags. All was silent, but with the words: "Class dismissed," twenty-six chairs scraped and the girls fled from the classroom amidst a cacophony of shouting voices.

"How was it?" Sharon asked, trying to make herself heard over the din.

"Not as bad as I expected," Nava replied.

"I told you it wouldn't be."

"But it was bad enough!"

"Did you leave any out?"

"Yes, number ten. I just could not remember which language is spoken in Brazil."

"Portuguese."

"Yes, I know — I remembered after I had put my pen down. Did you leave any out?"

"Number three: Which country has the largest population in the world?"

"China."

"Oh, no! You mean it was that easy? The first two questions were about China and I didn't even notice the clue."

"Never mind. Two more exams today and the first day will be over.

"Boy, will I be glad when they're all over."

Mrs. Jakovsky, in a white gown and cap, was ready to be wheeled into the operating room. Her eyes were moist with tears, but her face was full of courage. Chana Letchkov held her mother's hand as she received an injection.

"This will relax you, Mama. Please don't worry — I will be *davening* for you."

Mrs. Jakovsky just nodded. She seemed calmer already; the injection was starting to take effect.

"Chana, the best thing that you can do now is go home," Dr. Letchkov told his wife gently.

"Chaim, I must stay."

"But there is nothing that you can do here. We won't even know whether the operation has been successful or not until tomorrow when we remove the bandages. Look, it's almost three o'clock now; nursery school will be over soon. You just go and pick up Tikva, and try to go about your normal routine. I'll phone you as soon as the operation is finished."

"All right," she sighed. "I know you're looking after her, but I can't help worrying."

"I'll do the best I can for her," Dr. Letchkov said, "and I'll pray as well." Then he turned and walked down the corridor to the operating room. Chana Letchkov watched her mother being wheeled away down the long corridor. She wiped her eyes and pushed the elevator button.

Mrs. Letchkov and her children sat watching the silent telephone, willing it to ring.

"It's almost six o'clock," Ben-Zion informed them. "The operation should be over by now."

"Perhaps Papa has forgotten to call," Ari suggested.

"No. He said that he would, and he will keep his word," Mrs. Letchkov replied. Just then the phone rang and she rushed to pick up the receiver. "Hello? Yes...all right...I'll see you at about eight then...'bye."

"What did he say? What did he say?"

"He said that the operation went well, '*baruch Hashem. Babushka* is sleeping now and Papa will be home at about eight."

"When will we know if the operation was successful?"

"Not until tomorrow. They have to keep the bandages on for twenty-four hours." Mrs. Letchkov sighed. "Poor Mama, how I hope and pray that all will be well."

"*B'ezras Hashem* it will be," Ben-Zion comforted his mother.

"Two red cars!" Tikva cried happily, pointing out the car window. Nava sat in the back seat next to her little sister, playing a counting game with her in order to distract herself. She was apprehensive about going to the hospital, and only wanted to know that her grandmother was going to be all right. She found the tension in the car unbearable; it was so thick, she thought, that you could cut it with a knife. Her grandmother had especially asked for all of the family to be present when the bandages were removed, so that they could celebrate with her if the operation had been a success — or comfort her if it had failed.

Dr. Letchkov parked their car in the hospital parking lot, and they walked through the massive doors at the hospital entrance. The familiar scent of medicine and soap assailed Nava, and reminded her of visiting Chaya in the hospital. It was a smell which she usually liked, but which seemed ominous today.

"She is a little edgy," Dr. Letchkov warned the rest

of the family, "so try to keep her calm."

"How is she feeling otherwise?" Nava asked.

"Fine, but a bit groggy — you'll see."

The elevator door slid shut, and Nava watched the changing floor numbers light up on the panel above the heavy steel doors. At the sixth floor, a bell sounded and the doors slid open. They stepped out into the long, brightly-lit corridor and followed Dr. Letchkov to Mrs. Jakovsky's ward. Nurses walked briskly back and forth in their clean, starched uniforms, and the doctors all seemed to Nava to look like her father, in their white coats, with stethoscopes around their necks.

Nava experienced the same dread she had felt when she visited Chaya for the first time in the hospital. Her mother walked slowly, holding Tikva's hand, a short distance behind Nava. Her brothers followed silently, looking at the floor. Dr. Letchkov pushed open a swinging door to reveal a large, sunny four-bed ward. Nava searched the room anxiously for her grandmother, and gasped in horror as she spotted a woman whose whole face was covered in bandages.

"What's wrong?" her father whispered.

Nava pointed shakily at the woman.

"No, no, that's not *Babushka*. Here she is," he smiled, and led her to the bed in the corner by the window.

Nava slowly approached the bed, still trembling slightly from her fright. Ben-Zion took his mother's hand and led her gently. Avi walked with little Tikva, who studied her grandmother solemnly.

Mrs. Jakovsky lay there with her eyes bandaged.

Was she sleeping? Nava was concerned because her grandmother's face seemed expressionless, offering no clue as to how she was feeling.

"Hello!" Dr. Letchkov said cheerfully.

"Oh, hello, Chaim! Did you bring Chana and the children with you?" she asked weakly.

"Yes, yes, and they are all standing here."

"And little Tikva?"

"Yes, Tikva is here too. Are you ready?" Dr. Letchkov asked her.

"I suppose so," she sighed.

He turned to the nurse who was waiting in the doorway. "Mrs. Jakovsky is ready to have her bandages removed."

"Yes, Dr. Letchkov," she replied.

Nava did not know whether or not she should watch while her grandmother had her bandages taken off. What she really felt like doing was rushing from the room until it was all over. She tried to concentrate on the room instead of on her grandmother, taking in the drab walls, once white but now an uncertain gray; the metal cupboard in the corner, the large windows with flowery curtains. She watched the sunbeams on the starched white sheets.

Nava had to take a peep at what was happening. The Letchkov family stood mesmerized, waiting with bated breath as the nurse carefully removed the last of the bandages. Nava watched anxiously as her father gently placed a pair of dark glasses on her grandmother.

Slowly, her grandmother moved her head from side to side, while Dr. Letchkov, Mrs. Letchkov, Ben-

Zion, Ari, Nava and Tikva all watched silently and apprehensively. All at once she let out a sob, and Nava turned her head from the scene. The operation has not worked, she cried inwardly, struggling to keep herself under control. She could not bear her grandmother's pain; the prospect of the rest of her life shrouded in darkening shadows.

Then Nava heard a strange sound. *Babushka* was laughing! Laughing and crying, and turning excitedly in all directions. "Oh, my! I can't believe it! I can see so clearly!" She held out her arms to her daughter. Chana Letchkov and her mother laughed, embraced each other, cried with joy and then laughed again.

"Boris, it is a miracle!" Mrs. Jakovsky exclaimed. "Oh, what have I said? I mean *Chaim* — I was so excited that I forgot that we are living in freedom now, and can use our Hebrew names!"

"Yes," Chaim Letchkov replied, "you have liberty...and now you have health, too. But you must be careful," he added, assuming the tone of a physician and not a son-in-law. "Do not strain your eyes, keep those dark glasses on for six weeks, and do not lift anything heavy during that time."

"Yes, Doctor," Mrs. Jakovsky laughed, and gave both Nava and Tikva a massive hug.

17

"HEY, NAVA!" Rachel called as they all left the classroom after their last exam. "How did it go?"

"It wasn't bad," Nava replied, "but I'm so pleased that they are over. It is a great relief. Now I just want to know the results."

"I'm not sure I do! By the way, how is your grandmother?"

"*Barush Hashem*, she is fine, and improving every day. I forgot to tell you — she came home last night."

"Really? That's wonderful!"

"She is supposed to take it easy for the next four weeks, but the minute she came through the door, she headed straight for the kitchen — in her dark glasses —to help my Mother bake the *challos* for Shabbos."

"She sounds very determined!"

"Yes, she is very determined, independent and strong-willed. And she has a big soft spot for her grandchildren — she is kind, generous and spoils us rotten!"

"I must come around and meet her sometime."

"Yes, please do. She loves visitors. I must warn you, though: she speaks only Russian, Yiddish or *Ivrit* — no English."

"Well, that's all right. I can speak *Ivrit*."

"Do you know what happened last week? It was really funny. A neighbor of ours came to visit *Babushka* in the hospital, and didn't realize that she speaks no English. She spoke to my grandmother for about ten minutes before she realized that she had not understood a word."

"What did she do? Was she flustered or embarrassed?"

"A little, but she saw the funny side of it too. When I heard about it, though, I burst out laughing — I could just imagine my grandmother lying there, smiling and nodding her head politely at everything her visitor said!"

Rachel laughed. "I'll make sure that I don't make the same mistake."

"That's why I warned you! Well, I had better hurry home. My Dad told us that we must all make sure that she does not do too much."

"Will you be coming to group tomorrow?"

"Most probably."

"I'll see you there, then. Good Shabbos."

Nava arrived home humming a little tune softly to herself. She felt full of good cheer, happy simply to be alive. She was surprised to find her mother waiting for her at the gate; she had never done that before.

"Hi, Mama!" she called.

"Hello, Nava. Please come in right away. Papa is waiting to speak to all of you."

"All right. What is it? Is anything the matter?"

Nava went into the living room and sat down among the rest of the family. She and her brothers looked curiously from one to the other. Her father held a letter in his hand. Nava wondered what it could be about. Was she in some sort of trouble? Had she failed her tests? Did it have something to do with Russia?

"I received a letter this morning," Dr. Letchkov began, and then paused to look at each member of his family in turn. "It is from Doctor Shimoni, from Rofeh Cholim Hospital in Jerusalem. He wrote to tell me that Doctor Klein, unfortunately, had a sudden heart attack and died. *Baruch Dayan Ha-Emes.*"

"Doctor Klein...wasn't he the doctor that..."

"Yes, Nava — he was the doctor I was meant to succeed upon his retirement."

"What does all this mean then?" Ari asked.

"It means that we will be leaving for Israel much sooner than we expected," Dr. Letchkov replied.

"How much sooner?" Nava asked.

"We will be leaving on the second of August, *im yirtzeh Hashem.*"

"The second of August?" Avi and Ben-Tzion parroted. "How wonderful!"

"But today is already the second of July...a month! We will be leaving in exactly a month!"

"Yes, Nava."

Nava looked down at the floor, trying to conceal the

sudden tears which flooded her eyes. "I'd better start getting ready for Shabbos," she mumbled, and fled from the living room to the privacy of her own bedroom.

Nava was not sure how she felt about going to Israel so soon. Everything was happening too fast — it was all so confusing. Of course she was thrilled to finally be going to live in Jerusalem, but the suddenness overwhelmed her. She had always assumed that they would be in England for at least two years. She was overjoyed that she would not have to wait that long, but... it would mean starting a new school all over again and having to learn *Ivrit* properly — she knew *Ivrit* about as well as she had known English when they arrived in England. She thought of going through all the embarrassment and frustration again.

And all her good friends! She would have to leave them — how could she bear to say goodbye to them? They had already started making summer plans together. Nava was going to go to camp with them all. How could she tell them that she wouldn't be there?

There was a soft knock at her bedroom door. "Nava, may I come in?" her grandmother asked hesitantly.

"Yes, of course." Nava hastily wiped her tears.

Mrs. Jakovsky came in and sat down on the bed next to Nava. "Are you very upset about going on *aliyah*?"

"No, of course not, not really, but I just feel so confused. I am happy, but I'm also a little scared about what to expect. And what bothers me most..."

"Yes, Nava, I think I know."

"…is leaving my friends. I suppose that's really it. I'm going to miss them so much. First I had to leave Olga behind, and now my new friends."

"I understand."

"And I'm scared about…"

"About starting a new school all over again and trying to make new friends all over again?"

"Yes!"

"And trying to learn a new language. And you're probably worried that things may not be the way you expected them to be. And then, if you are unhappy, what if you should begin to wonder why you ever wanted to go to Israel in the first place, and then…you will feel guilty because here you are with exactly what you wanted — only now you don't seem to want it so much anymore. And all the while, you're thinking of all the people who long to go and would give anything to be in *Eretz Yisrael* but don't have the chance that you've been given."

"Yes! Yes! *Babushka*, how do you know? How do you know exactly what I am thinking?"

Her grandmother smiled and planted a kiss on Nava's tousled hair. "You forget, Nava, that I know you very well. And also that I have been through a few upheavals in my own life as well."

"Tell me then, how will I say goodbye to all my friends? How will I make friends all over again and learn *Ivrit*? And what if things *don't* work out?"

"You will think of a way to tell your friends. You will find the strength to do it, you will see."

"And do you think I'll be able to make such good friends in Israel?"

"Of course you will! Do you think Israeli girls are so

different from your friends here? And I'll tell you what — if you want, I will give you a few *Ivrit* lessons before we go."

"Oh, thank you, *Babushka*."

"You are very welcome, my Nava — and for a start, you can call me *Savta*. And as for things not working out — of course it may be difficult in the beginning, but as long as you think positively and don't expect too much, you will be fine. And one day you'll wonder why you ever felt unsure about it all."

"Oh, *Ba*...*Savta*, how do you know all this, if you have never been there?"

"Because I have lived and learned through experience. And besides that — even though I have never been to Israel, I somehow feel as though I know it already."

"I *do* feel excited, you know. I'll see Jewish people everywhere I go. It will be *our* country. I'll be living in *Yerushalayim*. I will be able to pray at the *Kosel*. I'll go to visit the north and the beautiful Gallilee, and visit *Yam Kinneres* and Safed, and the Golan Heights. I'll see the Negev, and the Judean Hills, and of course *Kever Rachel* and *Me'aras Ha-Machpelah*. Oh, there is so much I want to do when I get there! I can hardly believe it is about to come true."

"Well, I'm going to get ready for Shabbos," her grandmother said. "And you keep thinking about *Eretz Yisrael*. The more you think about it, the better it will seem."

"Nava, aren't you going to group this afternoon?" her mother asked the following day.

"No, I don't think so."

"Why not?"

"I just can't bring myself to tell everyone today that I'm leaving, and I know that if I see them I'll feel bad about not telling them."

Mrs. Letchkov nodded her head understandingly. "When are you going to tell them?"

"On Monday, in school."

"So, Nava, what is this important thing you have to tell us?" Sharon asked, settling herself on a bench in the playground. The girls all surrounded her, waiting expectantly.

Nava took a deep breath before beginning. "On Friday, my father received a letter from doctor Shimoni, from Rofeh Cholim Hospital in Jerusalem," she announced in one breath. "He wrote that Doctor Klein — the specialist my Dad was to succeed when he retired — died suddenly. This means," Nava continued softly, "that we will be leaving for Israel much sooner than we expected."

Nava's announcement was greeted by silence. Finally Sharon spoke. "When will you be leaving?"

"On the second of August."

"So soon? We knew it was coming, but we had no idea it would be this soon. It's such a surprise! I'm happy for you, but…" Rachel broke off.

"The second of August is a month away!" Chaya exclaimed.

"Yes," Nava replied, looking away from them.

"A month!"

"We're really going to miss you, Nava."

"I shall miss you, too," Nava answered, choking back her tears.

"You must write to us a lot," Chaya said.

"Of course I will."

"We will all write," Sharon replied.

"Nava, I am really happy for you. It's so wonderful that you are finally going to live in Israel," Naama said. "And I'm happy for me, too. At least I will still have one of my friends from England when I return home in December."

"I'm pleased for you, too," Rachel added, "and I'm not going to spend this month being sad and depressed. I'm going to be *happy* and make the most of you until the very last moment."

18

AS THE STADIUM BEGAN to fill up, Nava was amazed at how huge it looked. She could almost visualize a team of powerful athletes running around the track to the cries and cheers of the crowd, or a runner bearing a torch ascending the steps to light the Olympic flame. Chants could be heard all around the stadium, in support of the three school teams: "Yisrael!" "Akiva!" "Ezra!" Many people carried team banners which they waved as they chanted. Way down below her, Nava could see Rachel standing on the track at the starting line, doing some warm-up exercises in preparation for her first race, the 80-meter hurdles.

Rachel competed in three events that Sports Day: the 80-meter hurdles, the 200-meter sprint and the long jump. Being very athletic, this was the day she excelled. Nava herself was in the 800-meter sprint — having been roped into competing that very morning on the bus down to the stadium. Naama was in the high jump,

Sharon was in the three-legged race and Chaya was simply reporting on the events of the day for the school magazine — this was the only form her participation in sports took.

Rachel had concluded her warm-ups and now stood in position at the starting line. She and Sharon were on the "Yisrael" team, while Nava and Naama were with "Akiva." But the difference in teams never mattered to anyone; it was merely friendly rivalry. People often rooted for friends, even if they were on opposing teams.

The shouts died down and the only voice that could be heard belonged to the sports teacher, Mrs. Fielding.

"On your mark!" she called out firmly. "Get set!" The runners knelt down, ready to push themselves forward. "GO!" And with that, the shriek of her starting whistle echoed through the stillness of the air.

Rachel appeared to be flying down the course, taking the hurdles with such effortless grace that they seemed no obstacle at all.

"Rachel!" Nava, Sharon and Chaya cheered.

"She's winning!" Sharon shrieked. "Look at the distance between her and the rest of them."

Everyone in the stadium let out a cheer as Rachel crossed the finish line in triumph.

At lunchtime, all events halted for an hour. "Ezra" was in third place with one hundred points, "Akiva" was in second with one hundred and thirty-five, and "Yisrael" was first with one hundred and fifty points. Naama had brought "Akiva" a third-place win in the high jump.

"Nava, are you nervous about your race?" Chaya asked.

"No, not really, but I am sure I will be when I am actually standing at the starting line. I have never done anything like this before!"

"You'll be just fine."

"I am glad that *you* are so sure," Nava joked.

"All girls participating in the three-legged race, please come down to the track now," Mrs. Fielding called into her megaphone.

"Looks like it's my turn to go now," Sharon said. "This is going to be great fun."

Sharon joined Michal — her partner — down on the track and they tied their legs together with the scarf which Mrs. Fielding handed to them. Sharon looked up at her friends and made a thumbs-up sign before hobbling along with Michal to the starting line. There, Sharon took one look at the four other pairs participating in the race and began to giggle.

"Calm down, Sharon," Mrs. Fielding said, but it was too late — by that time her contagious laughter had spread to the other pairs as well. "Control yourselves. I am starting the race now; this is very serious."

"Serious?" one girl asked. "It's only a three-legged race," and with that, they all collapsed in another fit of laughter.

"On your mark!" Mrs. Fielding called. "Get set! Go!"

Sharon and Michal started out in a half-run, half-jog. As Michal was far taller than Sharon and much faster, she practically dragged Sharon along. Poor Sharon couldn't manage to keep up, and suddenly tripped and went sprawling across the track, carrying Michal with her. Since they were so tangled, they couldn't stand up in time and watched helplessly as the four other pairs crossed the finishing line.

"What a joke!" Michal said.

"For you, yes. You absoutely dragged me down the track," Sharon replied good-humoredly.

"And you threw me right across it."

"We're some team," laughed Sharon. "It's lucky we didn't enter a serious race. We couldn't even finish a fun one."

"Come on, let's get untangled. The last race is starting any minute now."

"The 800-meter?"

"Yes. Nava's in it, and I must watch it."

Nava stood at the starting line and began to get nervous. With all three teams almost even in the standings, the whole competition depended on this race. She was sure that when Mrs. Fielding gave the starting signal, she'd somehow miss it and be left behind in the dust. The stadium grew quiet and Nava stood erect, facing straight ahead. Mrs. Fielding gave the starting signal, raised her whistle to her lips and blew. Nava heard the shrill sound of the whistle and began to run.

Go easy, she told herself, and keep it steady. She jogged consistently, pacing herself as she went, but soon noticed that she was lagging behind; the other five runners had overtaken her and were leading by as much as thirty meters. Halfway around the track on her first lap, she was already feeling tired. Her heart was beating so hard that she could hear it pounding in her brain.

By the time she'd completed her first lap, Nava was exhausted. She wasn't used to such exertion and felt almost ready to give up. The other competitors were way ahead of her. Then all at once she heard a shout: "Come on, Nava!" She couldn't tell who it was, but it gave her enough encouragement to continue another few steps. "Come on, Nava!" Worn out and panting, but with a great deal of fight still left in her, she somehow persevered for another lap. She wasn't ready to give up so easily.

"Nava! Nava!" It seemed as if everyone in the stadium was cheering her on. She felt her pace quicken, and steadily she overtook two girls, with half a lap to go. Her fatigue seemed to melt away.

"We want Nava!" She outdistanced another two girls and was almost neck-and-neck with Shuli, who was in the lead. Nava seemed to be flying effortlessly.

"Nava!" There were twenty paces to go.

"It's going to be a tie!" Sharon yelled over the din to Michal.

Nava took two fantastic leaps and was over the finish line one split second ahead of Shuli.

"She won!" Naama shouted, and ran down to Nava, who was sitting on the track, already encircled by friends, clearly exhausted, but enjoying her moment of glory as the cheers echoed around the stadium.

Within a minute, Nava found herself surrounded by all her classmates. Someone handed her a drink, which she accepted gratefully. Then they hoisted her onto their shoulders and carried her back to her seat in triumph. Down below, Mrs. Fielding completed the scoreboard: "Ezra": two hundred and fifty points; "Yisrael": three hundred and ten points; and "Akiva": three hundred and fifteen points!

Everybody in "Akiva" let out a cheer and many team members came over to congratulate Nava. "What a performance! If it weren't for you," someone from an older class said to her, "we never would have won."

This was a day she would never forget.

"Michal, would you come in please?" Mrs. Gera said.

"Wish me luck," Michal whispered to her friends as she turned and followed Mrs. Gera into the office.

It was Results Day.

Nava waited patiently outside the office, knowing that her turn was next. She promised herself not to panic unless her marks were really dreadful. The teachers had told her not to worry too much about her grades, since she was bound to find the language difficult and she had also missed more than half the year's work. Still, she was concerned.

The office door reopened and Michal came out clutching her envelope.

"Nava, would you come in please?" Mrs. Gera called from inside.

Nava rose slowly from her seat.

"Good luck," Michal whispered to Nava as she went through the door. Nava acknowledged it with a slight nod.

"Well, Nava," Mrs. Gera began, "I must say you did very well indeed, considering how short a time you have been here. You may have one or two disappointments, but that is to be expected. On the whole, though, I am sure that you will be very pleased."

"Thank you." Nava took the envelope which Mrs. Gera handed to her and hastily left he office. She felt much calmer now, after hearing that she had done well. She opened her envelope and scanned her results:

Geography — C	Computers — B
History — C	*Ivrit* — C
English — D	*Chumash* — B
Math — A	*Nach* — B
Physics — B	*Dinim* — B
Chemistry — A	Jewish History — C

Nava could not believe what she saw, and reread her report card to make sure she had not misunderstood. She had succeeded!

A few minutes later she found Sharon in the hall, studying her own results.

"How did you do?" Nava asked her.

"Three C's, two B's and seven A's."

"Wow!"

"What did you get?" Nava showed Sharon her results. "Nava, that is fantastic! An A in Math, and in Chemistry too."

Nava felt a little embarrassed and was unsure of what to reply. "But *you* are brilliant at languages," she told Sharon.

"They are about the only subjects I like! How about you?"

"Well, I really like all the subjects, but I am not brilliant in any of them." Nava suddenly smiled to herself, recalling that long-ago first day at Batsheva, when she had vowed to work as hard as possible. She felt the glow of achievement.

19

THERE WAS A FRENZY of activity in
Form Three. Desks were being tipped over and emptied
of the last remnants of eraser shavings, pencil sharpen-
ings and peanut butter sandwich crumbs which clung
stubbornly to the inner corners of the desks. A cassette
of Hebrew songs was being played at full blast — this
was the only day of the year that cassettes were allowed
in the classroom, and the girls were making the most of
it. Aliza was busy removing the posters from the wall.
Slowly the classroom was becoming an empty shell,
ready for next year's class to fill it with its own character.

Nava joined in the fun, trying to keep up her spirits,
though everything made her feel sad, and this sadness
infused even the smallest things with sentimental value.
Clearing out her desk, she found an old, crumpled piece
of paper. She was about to tear it up and throw it away
when her curiosity got the better of her and she decided
to take a quick look. It turned out to be a note Sharon

had smuggled to her, soon after she had first arrived at school.

Dear Nava,
How are you finding our English class? Don't you think the book we are reading is boring? Are you having any problems with it? Look at Rachel. I think she's falling asleep. What do you think?
Love, Sharon.

Nava winced when she read her own reply, written in broken English, the best she could write then.

Dear Sharon,
I like story but English quite hard. You are rite, Rachel falls asleep, her eys now are closd. I hope she get not in troble.
Love, Nava.

She decided to keep it as a souvenir, and folded it up carefully before slipping it into her pocket.

"How are you doing?" Sharon asked as she passed Nava's desk carrying a bag of papers to the wastebasket.

"Okay. Look what I found, Sharon — do you remember this?" She handed the note to Sharon, who read it quickly and gave a laugh.

"Yes, I do. And do you remember when Mrs. Banks *did* discover that Rachel was sleeping? She called on her and asked her to describe what was happening in the chapter we were discussing..."

"Yes, and Rachel just looked at her and said, 'I'm

sorry, but I don't know. I fell asleep.'"

"At least she was honest."

"Nava!" Naama called. "Could you come over here? We want to take some pictures."

After the photo session, everyone trooped down to the assembly. Nava blinked back tears as she realized that this was to be her last assembly ever at Batsheva High. Everybody in school had become like one big happy family to her, in a way she would never have thought possible.

Following the *davening*, Mrs. Gera rose to make her speech. "This year has been an excellent one," she began. "Our fourth annual trip to Israel was a great success and I know that besides having a lot of fun, the girls who participated learned a great deal. We hope they will all continue to correspond with their new Israeli friends.

"The Drama Club's Purim play was also very successful, and I received many letters from people saying how much they enjoyed the performance. In fact, one woman wrote that it was done so professionally that she almost thought she was in a real theater."

The girls clapped, and Mrs. Gera continued. "Through the Purim performance and our other projects, we raised a large amount of money for *tzedakah* this year. I would like to call upon Tamar, who has chaired the *tzedakah* committee, to tell us how much was raised."

Tamar left her seat and walked up to the stage. "I am delighted to announce that this year our school raised five thousand pounds altogether, with the second-year class raising the greatest amount. The money will be distributed to various *tzedakah* projects both here and in Israel." The audience clapped once again, and Tamar returned to her seat.

"Thank you, Tamar." Mrs. Gera now turned to her audience and smiled broadly. "Last week we said good-bye to the upper sixth form, and the week before, it was the fifth form's final assembly. Today, I would like you all to join me in saying goodbye to a very special member of our student body, Nava Letchkov, who is leaving us to go on *aliyah*. Although Nava has been with us only a short while, she has made her mark on all of us and there will always be a special place for her here. Nava, please come up to the stage."

Nava felt embarrassed and self-conscious about standing there in front of the whole school. She had never been up on stage in the assembly before.

Mrs. Gera shook Nava's hand warmly and handed her a book. "Nava, I would like to present this to you on behalf of all of us. We wish you and your family *hatzla-chah rabbah* in *Eretz Yisrael*. We are all going to miss you."

"Thank you," Nava whispered, and walked back to her seat carefully carrying her brand new *siddur*. It had a silver cover with semi-precious stones set in, and was engraved with her name. It was exquisite.

Assembly continued with a presentation of the Sports Cup to the captain of the "Akiva" team for winning on Sports Day, and Nava was called up to the stage once again, to collect her gold medal along with the other girls who had come in either first, second or third in one of the competitions.

Once they were dismissed, Nava went to the staff room to say goodbye to a few of her teachers, and then hurried back to her classroom to see it for the last time and bid goodbye to her friends.

"Nava — smile," someone called out as she walked into class; she looked up in time to see a bright flash. "Thanks," Michal said, waving her camera. Nava collected her last few belongings together and crammed them into her bag.

"I hope we'll still be able to see each other before you go," Chaya said.

I'm sure we'll be able to — I still have another two weeks."

"We can try and get together after *Tisha B'Av*, and go somewhere really lovely."

"That sounds great. I'm only sorry that I won't see all of you together again before I go."

Sharon gave a little smile. "Perhaps one day," she mused.

"Yes, one day," Nava replied ruefully.

"You won't forget to write, will you?" Rachel asked.

"Of course not!"

"Where will you be living?" Naama asked.

"Didn't I tell you?" Nava suddenly glowed. "In *Yerushalayim*."

"Really? Then we'll be neighbors! I live in Jerusalem too, in the Jewish Quarter of the Old City."

"Near the *Kosel?*"

"Yes — I can take you there. It's only about a five minute walk from my house."

"How does it feel to be about to live in Israel, Nava?" Michal asked.

"It seems almost unreal, but I am really excited. At the beginning I felt a little scared about having to build up a new life all over again, but eventually I came to the conclusion that if I have done it once, I can do it again."

The dismissal bell rang. "Well," Nava sighed, "I suppose this is it." She picked up her bag and took one long, last look at her classroom; after so many hours spent there, it had become almost like a second home to her. She knew she had to go, but somehow she could not make herself leave the classroom. She stood in the center of the room absorbing every detail, until they were all indelibly printed in her memory. Then she closed her eyes. "I'm ready."

The whole of Form Three left the building together in one large group. Nava couldn't help thinking what a contrast this was to the day she had first arrived at Batsheva. Then she had walked alone, studying all the other girls strolling into school together, and wondering if she would ever feel like one of them. She had come so far since that day.

When they reached the gates she said goodbye to her friends, hugging each and every one of them in turn. She was overcome by emotion; tears streamed down her cheeks unchecked. "Goodbye," she wept. "I will never forget you, never ever."

Nava turned and slowly walked away.

20

CHANA LETCHKOV CLOSED UP the last of the packing cartons. "Well, that's it," she said to Nava.

"Is there nothing more to do?" Nava asked.

"No, nothing."

"Can I —"

"Why don't you —" Nava and her mother spoke simultaneously.

"You first," her mother smiled.

"No, what were you going to say?" Nava asked.

"I was going to say, why don't you call up a friend and do something together? After all, it's your last day, and since we've finished all the packing, you have time to do whatever you like."

Nava gave a laugh. "I was just going to say that since we were finished with everything, could I call up a friend?"

It was her mother's turn to laugh. "Well, you know the answer already. Go ahead."

Nava dialed Sharon's number and heard the familiar voice on the other end of the line.

One Good Turn

"Hi, Sharon! It's Nava. Listen, all the packing is finished, so I was wondering, are you free to do anything today?"

There was a brief silence and then Sharon replied hastily, "I'm really sorry, but I won't be able to."

"Oh…oh, well, goodbye then."

Rachel stretched out on a comfortable lounge chair in the garden and lazily glanced at her watch. It was only ten-thirty, and there was plenty of time yet for the girls to do everything they had to do. Ten-thirty on Sunday morning, the first of August. Today was *the* day, Rachel thought to herself and smiled. How would she wait patiently for evening to arrive?

"Rachel, telephone!" Mrs. Nachshon called.

"Coming," Rachel replied, hurrying into the house and picking up the phone. "Hello?"

"Hi, Rachel, it's me, Chaya," she said with urgency.

"Oh hi, what's up?"

"Nava."

"What do you mean?"

"She phoned me, wanting to do something today, and then Sharon telephoned to say that she had called her as well. Of course I told her I wasn't able to do anything today, but I feel so bad — I mean, it is her last day. I can just imagine how she's feeling."

"In that case, I'll ring her now."

"Thanks."

"Mama, it's really strange. Everyone I've phoned seems to be busy today."

"Oh?" Mrs. Letchkov answered, and swiftly turned

131

away, busying herself with something unimportant.

"I suppose I phoned a bit late," Nava continued. "Everyone has probably made arrangements for this and that already. It's a lovely day and people want to get out. I guess I can't expect them to be sitting inside waiting for me to call."

"Did you try Rachel?"

"Yes, but I can't get through."

"Hm-m."

"Maybe I'll ask *Savta* to give me another *Ivrit* lesson."

Just then the telephone rang, and Nava ran to answer it. "Hello?"

"Hi, Nava, it's Rachel. I was wondering, would you like to come over for dinner this evening?"

"Oh, yes, I'd love to. That would be very nice. Can you hold on while I ask my mother?"

A moment later, she was back on the line. "Rachel? My mother says I may go."

"Super! Shall we make it at about six?"

"That's fine."

"See you then!"

Shortly after six that evening, Nava stood on Rachel's front porch and rang the doorbell. Mrs. Nachshon answered the door.

"Hello, Nava. Please come in. I'll go and tell Rachel that you're here." Strange, Nava mused, Mrs. Nachshon is not usually that formal. A few moments passed, and Nava was still standing alone in the hall. The house seemed unusually quiet.

At last Rachel appeared from the kitchen, looking flushed and excited. "Hi, Nava," she greeted her warmly. "Come in. I thought that we'd eat in the garden this evening since it's so warm outside. What do you think?"

"That sounds lovely," Nava replied, following her friend.

They walked through the kitchen, and Rachel slowly pushed open the back door which led to the garden, beckoning to Nava to come out.

"SURPRISE!"

All of a sudden there was a huge bang and streamers flew everywhere. Nava watched in a daze as her whole class emerged from hiding places all over the large garden.

"Surprise! Surprise!"

Nava was overwhelmed and speechless. Rachel switched on a cassette of lively Israeli folk music, and Mr. Nachshon switched on a string of colored light bulbs he'd strung in the yard.

"How do you feel?" Rachel asked, squeezing her arm affectionately.

"Happy, sad, surprised — I don't know! Mostly wonderful. But Rachel, when did you plan all this?"

"We've been planning it for weeks. Tell me really, didn't you suspect anything?"

"Not in the least. Thinking back, though, I remember when I was talking to Chaya about not seeing you all together again, and I noticed that Sharon had a mysterious smile on her face."

"I nearly ruined it, didn't I?" Sharon said.

"No, no, because I only now realize why you were smiling then."

"When you said that to Chaya, I didn't know how to contain myself. I thought I was going to blurt it all out!"

"But you didn't! And you know, my mother was acting rather strangely this morning. Did she know about this too?"

"How did you guess?

"And then, you were all busy today. Chaya had so many important things to do!"

Chaya grinned. "Well, it was perfectly true. I had a great deal to do today...which you'll soon see!"

Just then, a flash of color on the wall of the house caught Nava's eye and she turned around to look. There, strung from one top window to the other was a huge poster declaring in fluorescent colors: WE'LL MISS YOU NAVA.

"Oh, it's beautiful," Nava breathed. "Who made it?"

"I did," grinned Chaya. "That was one of the things I was busy with this morning."

Mrs. Nachshon came into the garden. "Anybody hungry?" she asked, all the previous formality gone now.

"Yes, I think we'll eat now," Rachel said. "I'll help you bring everything out."

"I'll join you," Chaya said.

"And I too," Nava added, following Chaya and Rachel.

"Oh, no!" Rachel exclaimed. "This is your special night. You just stay here and enjoy yourself."

Within a few moments the garden was transformed into a colorful open-air restaurant. Folding tables were set up and a buffet of *pittah*, *falafel*, *techinah* and salads was laid out. Chaya spread out blankets for them to sit on, picnic style.

"Rachel, what are these?" Nava asked, pointing to one of the plates.

"They're called *felafel* balls," Rachel replied, "and you had better get used to them, because you'll be having them a lot in Israel."

Nava picked one off the plate and took a small bite. "Mmmm," she said, "these are very good."

"Oh, Nava!" Rachel burst out." Things won't be the same here without you. But even though I'm going to miss you terribly, I am so happy for you that you're finally going to fulfill the dream of living in *Eretz Yisrael*."

"You will come and visit me in Israel sometime, won't you, Rachel?"

"Of course, *im yirtzeh Hashem*. And who knows, I may have the *zechus* of living there one day too. Oh, and before I forget, I want to give you this." Rachel withdrew a small, neatly wrapped package from her pocket and handed it to Nava.

Nava, visibly moved, opened the package with trembling fingers. Inside was a stunning gold *Magen David* pendant on a delicate gold chain.

"Rachel," Nava whispered, "this is beautiful. Thank you. I shall wear it always."

"Presentation time!" Chaya called. "Nava, please come and sit down in the place of honor — a beautiful …um…deck chair," she joked. Then, her face becoming serious, she said, "On behalf of us all I would like to present you with this album of photos and mementos to remind you of your few months here with us."

"Don't tell me," Nava joked, in an attempt to cover up the emotions which threatened to engulf her, "you made it this morning."

"You said it!"

Rachel swtiched the volume up on the cassette recorder. "Come on everybody," she called. "Let's dance!"

Half an hour later, they all flopped down onto the blankets. Michal brought out her guitar, and Rachel her small accordion, and they began to play their favorite, familiar songs.

The sun had almost set, and Nava was reminded of a scene quite similar to this, which had taken place only a few months before when they'd been singing around the campfire together at Tree-Glade. She remembered how tranquil it had all been, and then — minutes later — the panic as everyone searched desperately for Chaya. She recalled her tears of frustration, as she blamed herself for what had happened, and her terrible fear for Chaya's safety. The search party, finding Chaya, the joy and the relief.

She remembered her first day at school — how she had been so shy — and meeting Rachel and all her other friends for the first time. And then the day they received the letter from her grandmother about how she would need the eye operation. The letters, the petitions, the *Tehillim* chain. The dreadful day she heard that her grandmother had disappeared, and the glorious night her grandmother appeared on their doorstep. The operation and its successful outcome. Exams, Sports Day, her final assembly...and now this evening.

All this would be etched in her memory forever.

She was sorry that Olga had never had the chance to meet all her wonderful new friends, but perhaps one day she still would. Olga, Nava thought, you were right. It is happening, just the way you said it would. One day soon we will be together in *Eretz Yisrael.*

Nava smiled as she looked around at all her dear friends singing together, and savored the last few precious moments which she had to share with them.

Epilogue

THE PLANE BEGAN to make its descent. With the song "*Hevenu Shalom Aleichem*" playing softly in the background, Nava caught her first glimpse of the Holy Land. With every passing moment, she could see more clearly the vibrant colors of her beckoning homeland: the deep, sapphire blue of the Mediterranean; its golden coastline; the vivid, red tile roofs; the gleaming white stone of the buildings. She knew that here at last she could let the endless gray of her years in Russia fade into distant memory.

The plane landed and the passengers rushed to collect their baggage and disembark as quickly as possible. Nava and her family, though, lingered behind, wanting to prolong every second of their first few moments in *Eretz Yisrael*.

Nava stepped out of the airplane and looked around her. It was early in the morning, and the blue sky and rich earth were suffused with the sun's glow. She inhaled the sweet air of *Eretz Yisrael* and slowly walked down the stairs onto its precious, holy soil.

Glossary

The following glossary provides a partial explanation of some of the foreign words and phrases used in this book. The spelling and explanations reflect the way the specific word is used herein. Often, there are alternate spellings and meanings for the words.

ALIYAH: lit., ascent; immigration to Israel.

BARUCH HASHEM: "Thank God."

BAS MITZVAH: a Jewish girl of 12, the age at which she assumes her religious obligations.

BENTCH: (Y.) to recite the Grace after Meals.

B'EZRAS HASHEM: "With God's help."

CHALLOS: braided Sabbath loaves.

CHAS V'SHALOM: "God forbid!"

CHUMASH: the Pentateuch.

DAVEN: (Y.) to pray.

DINIM: Torah laws.

ERETZ YISRAEL: the Land of Israel.

EREV SHAVUOS: the eve of the Festival of **SHAVUOS.**

HAGGADAH: the story of the Jews' redemption from Egypt, read during the **SEDER** on **PESACH.**

HATZLACHAH RABBAH: lit., much success; "Good luck!"

HEVENU SHALOM ALEICHEM: "We have brought you peace," the refrain of a popular song of welcome.

IM YIRTZEH HASHEM: "God willing."

IVRIT: Hebrew.

KEVER RACHEL: Rachel's Tomb.

KOSEL HA-MA'ARAVI: The Western Wall.

LAG BA-OMER: the festive 33rd day in the 49-day period of semi-mourning between **PESACH** and **SHAVUOS**.

LASHON HA-RA: malicious gossip.

MADRICHAH: a counselor.

MAGEN DAVID: lit., the shield of David, the "Jewish star."

ME'ARAS HA-MACHPELAH: the Cave of Machpelah in Hevron, burial place of the Patriarchs.

MODEH ANI: "I thank," the opening words of the prayer recited upon awakening.

PESACH: the Festival of Passover.

REFUAH SHELEMAH: "A complete recovery!"

SEDER: the order of the **PESACH** night ceremony recalling the Exodus from Egypt and the liberation from bondage.

SE'UDAH SHELISHIS: the third Sabbath meal.

SHALOM ALEICHEM: "Peace be with you," a traditional Jewish greeting.

SHAVUOS: the Festival celebrated seven weeks after **PESACH**, commemorating the giving of the Torah at Mount Sinai.

SHUL: (Y.) a synagogue.

SIDDUR: a prayer book.

TEFILLAH: prayer.

TEFILLAS HA-DERECH: the traveler's prayer.

TEHILLIM: Psalms.

TISHA B'AV: the Ninth of Av, a day of mourning commemorating the destruction of the First and Second Temples.

TZEDAKAH: charity; righteousness.

YAM KINNERES: the Sea of Galilee.

YERUSHALAYIM: Jerusalem.

YOM TOV: a Jewish Festival.

ZECHUS: a privilege; merit.